GALACTIC MAIL
Revolution!

by

RICHARD F. WEYAND

RICHARD F. WEYAND

ISBN 978-09970709-9-6
Printed in the United States of America

Credits
Front Cover: Oleg Volk
Model: Katherine Nichols
Back Cover Photo: Oleg Volk

Published by Weyand Associates, Inc.
Bloomington, Indiana, USA
February, 2018

CONTENTS

RICHARD F. WEYAND

Family Legacy

Emily Gunderson sat in a rocking chair on the big front porch of Campbell Hall, the large stone house her grandfather, Maximillian Childers Campbell, had built in the hills overlooking the city of New Hope on the planet Horizon almost a hundred years before. Her attention was not on the stunning view of the city and the valley in which it lay, however. Instead she watched her great, great grandchildren playing in the yard that sloped gradually away from the house toward the tree line below.

With her sat her great grandchild, Pamela Lieber, the mother of three of the young children cavorting below. They were all together here at the big house for Founders Day, the annual holiday celebrating the founding of the colony, a hundred and twenty years ago this year.

"Pamela, dear."

"Yes, Grandma Gunderson?"

"I need to tell you a story, so that it not be lost."

"You should write it down," Pam said.

"No. This story can never be written down. You must promise me that, my dear. That you will never write it down, but that you, too, will pass it on to one of your great grandchildren when your time grows short. It is a story I was told by my own great grandmother, Grandma Childers, almost seventy years ago, when I was about the age you are now."

Emily had Pam's attention now. Grandma Childers was a legend on Horizon, but not for her incredible military career, or for the founding and early leadership of Galactic Mail, but for Childers House. Stir-crazy in her retirement, and seeing a need, Jan Childers had founded and run the charity that ensured that no orphan, no widow, no veteran on Horizon was ever abandoned to their own meager resources. If you were down and out, Childers House was there for you. It never turned anyone away. Initially funded by Childers herself, those who had benefitted and turned around their lives, and those who believed in its mission, saw to it that it remained well-funded. It was celebrating the one hundredth anniversary of its founding this year.

1

Emily gripped Pam's arm, on the arm of the rocker next to hers, and looked her in the eye.

"Can you promise me that, Pamela? That you will pass on the story, never write it down, see to it that it is carried on?"

"Yes, Grandma Gunderson. I promise."

"Good, good."

Emily patted Pam's arm, settled back in her chair.

"It begins before Grandma Childers moved here to Horizon, when she was running Galactic Mail...."

Safety Play

Jan Childers, Bill Campbell, Tien Jessen, Jeanette Xi, and Jake Durand were meeting in a secure conference room in the headquarters building of Galactic Mail on the planet Doma. It was three years since the founding of Galactic Mail, and the operation was finally fully up and running. Childers was CEO, Campbell, her husband, was head of Intelligence and Security, Jessen was head of Operations, and Xi was vice president. Durand had retired as head of the Intelligence Division of the Commonwealth Space Force, and moved to Doma for his retirement. He was there as a consultant.

"The reason I wanted to get together is to address one big concern that keeps gnawing at me," Childers said. "I don't know what to do about it yet, and I want you all to think about it.

"We need a safety play. A reset button, if you will. What happens if all this–" Childers waved her hand around in the air – "goes off the rails? Becomes a government? Becomes a tyranny? How do we reset it? How do we – from the grave – reassert control and get it back on its mission? Assume we need to do it twice. The first time, according to our estimates, is probably in a hundred and fifty years or so. How do we do that?

"I don't want to talk about it today. I want you to think about it. I want to meet every other week to discuss it until we solve it. No notes, nobody else involved. We need a plan first.

"How do we, a hundred and fifty years from now, after we're all dead and buried, recognize the problem, kick out the rats, and restore this institution to its proper mission?"

"You basically want to build in a revolution," Durand said.

"Correct. The big questions are, How do we know when a revolution is necessary, and, How do we ensure it succeeds?"

"So you've had a couple of weeks to think about it. Let's kick it around a little bit and see where we are," Childers said.

"I think the first obvious thing is that it has to be something outside the organization. A hundred and fifty years is too long for

3

organizational solutions. It would allow someone too much time to figure out how to disable whatever mechanism we come up with. It has to be something the rats don't know is there, that has the element of surprise," Durand said.

"Which implies an organization outside the organization. Have we just moved the problem one layer deeper? Who watches the watchers?" Bill asked.

"The first thing you did to keep it from becoming a government is to use a different organizational structure, the corporation. How about another organizational structure to keep an eye on it?" Xi asked.

"What kind of organizational structure?" Childers asked.

"Family," Xi said.

"You mean a family legacy sort of deal? Each person passes it on to someone in the next generation?" Bill asked.

"Probably more like two or three generations, but yeah," Xi said. "As each watcher grows old, they pass it on to one member of the young adult generation. That reduces the wander in the story."

"They can also pick who among their great grandchildren are the most stable, the most mature, the most reasonable people," Childers said.

"You're going to have people die prematurely, though. The story will be lost," Durand said.

"We can start multiple chains. If each of us tells two of our great grandchildren, we would have ten chains going forward. We can calculate the individual odds of those being broken, come up with some expectations about how many of the chains survive for a given time period," Jessen said.

"That's only eight chains going forward. Jan and I will have the same family links," Bill said.

"We can bring in some others, until we have the numbers we want," Jan said. "So how would this work?"

"Some number of them have to agree things are off the rails," Bill said.

"Then how do we keep this new group from taking over whenever they want?"

"They don't have to each know about the others. They can think they're the only ones," Xi said.

"Or at least not know who the others are," Durand said.

"That would work as well," Xi said.

"How do they vote then?" Bill asked.

"Mail. Simplest way. When one thinks it's off the rails, they send a mail. If the system gets so many mails, it kicks in," Jessen said.

"How do we keep the mailbox from being discovered?" Durand asked.

"Some sort of password system. If the password is in the mail, then it gets through. If not, you get a 'no such mailbox' reply," Jessen said.

"It's got to be a password that can be remembered, but not written down. We don't want anything written down," Childers said.

"Some string from a document or a book would work. You just have to remember which book," Bill said.

"OK, so. We have our watchers, and the required number send their mails. Now what happens?" Jan asked.

"Well, it has to be computerized, or you need another organization to carry it out," Jessen said.

"Agreed. But what are computer systems going to be like in a hundred and fifty years? How can you write something now that will run on whatever it is?" Durand asked.

"We could write it in COBOL," Childers said.

"In what?" Durand asked.

"Sorry. Very old Earth joke," Childers said.

"Actually, there's probably a way to do this," Jessen said. "You can't upgrade every computer at once in a big network. No matter how much the technology changes, you have to be able to accommodate other versions. That's where trans-compilers come in."

"Trans-compilers?" Xi asked.

"Yes, a software program that translates code to a new system. It processes existing source code to generate new source code for the new system, then compiles it to run on the new system," Jessen said.

"But won't it be obvious what the source code does?" Bill asked.

"No. Trans-compiled source code is basically unreadable. What we do is write the code in a previous generation system, then trans-compile it to the current systems. It's just part of what we use, at that point. Nobody will be able to decipher it. We'll embed it in the system, and they'll just keep trans-compiling it forward," Jessen said.

"And storage? Protection against a completely new system?" Childers asked.

"We'll build it like a virus. It will always try to handshake with itself in the systems it talks to. If it doesn't see itself, it will replicate itself. We can also embed it in the ships. The hyperspace engine computer code is what calculates the gravitational stresses and the transition points. Nobody wants to mess with that. I'll have to look into it a bit, but we should be OK," Jessen said.

"And we'll be able to test this?" Childers asked.

"Oh, yes. No way I'm going to rely on untested code. We should be able to set up a closed environment and test it."

"All right, so assuming we can do all that, what does the code do?" Childers asked.

"Stops obeying orders from the powers that be, and takes orders from the family members, I would guess," Durand said.

"Whatever we do, though, doesn't it have to be in line with the corporate by-laws? To be legal?" Bill asked.

"Go read the immutable portion of the by-laws again," Childers said.

"This really has been bothering you for a long time, hasn't it?" Durand asked.

"Oh, yes. It's in there. Couched in legal gobbledygook, but it's in there," Childers said.

It was two years before Jessen was able to report: "It's done."

"The code is in there?" Childers asked.

"Yes, and it's replicating itself throughout Galactic Mail."

"And how many are in the inner circle now?"

"Twelve counting you and Bill only once," Jessen said.

"So we'll have twenty-four chains going forward."

"Correct. And the odds are we'll still have twenty at one hundred and fifty years."

"We've done what we could," Childers said. "I hope it works."

The Legacy Continues

"... and that's the story my great grandmother Emily Gunderson told me almost seventy years ago, my dear, on this very porch" Pamela Lieber said.

Her great granddaughter Patricia Dawson looked at her with wide eyes.

"That's unbelievable, Grandma Lieber. That was how many years ago now, that Grandma Childers put in her safety mechanism?"

"Oh, let's see. It was about ten years before she moved here, and she moved here when she was sixty years old. And Grandma Childers has been dead now, what? Almost a hundred and twenty years, I think. At age one hundred and five. So that would make it a hundred and seventy years or so? I think that's right."

"And it's never been needed," Dawson said.

"Not yet. But you need to keep watch, my dear. You need to keep the watch. My time on guard is over now."

"And what is the mailbox, and what is the password?"

"The mailbox is simple enough. Jan Childers at Galactic Mail. Send mail there, and unless it contains the password, you'll get a message back that there's no such mailbox."

"And the password?"

"Grandma Childers was a student of history, Patty. There is an old Earth document that was one of her favorites, called the Declaration of Independence. There are two hundred and two words, beginning with "We hold these truths to be self-evident" that she considered the most important words ever written in any language. Any twelve consecutive words from those two hundred and two can be used as the password, except the last twenty-two words."

"What are the last twenty-two words, Grandma Lieber?"

"They're your vote that Galactic Mail is off track, that it has spiraled into despotism. Those words are "it is their right, it is their duty, to throw off such government, and to provide new guards for their future security." Send those words to Grandma Childers' mailbox, and, once enough of your fellow Watchers agree, the leadership of Galactic Mail will be overthrown."

"Overthrown?" Dawson asked.

"None of the computers will obey the leadership. Their computer accounts will be frozen. None of the ships will obey their orders. The ships' captains will get secret orders not to obey them. Instead, they will all obey you and your fellow Watchers. And you will have secret instructions waiting as well."

"That's – I don't know what that is. That's incredible. That twenty-four people, spread around the galaxy, can just flip the switch."

"The power of Galactic Mail being in the wrong hands is a terrible prospect, Patty. It's what Grandma Childers was most worried about, all those years ago," Gunderson said. "Now, you need to send a message to the mailbox, just the password and 'Childers 2', so the computer knows you are the new Watcher in this chain, and knows where to find you."

"I'll do that right now."

"Please do, dear."

Dawson pulled out her comp, found the ancient text, selected twelve words, added 'Childers 2,' and mailed them to Jan Childers at Galactic Mail.

"Done," Dawson said.

Lieber sighed, and sank back in her chair.

She had not broken the chain.

A Voice From The Past

The acknowledgement to Patty Dawson's mail message to Jan Childers' mailbox at Galactic Mail came in return mail the next day. It was a huge VR file. With the twins off at pre-school, she had time to log into the VR system and open it.

She found herself in a full-immersion VR, on the porch of Campbell Hall, looking out over New Hope. The ancient stone house looked relatively new, while the bustling modern city she was used to was little more than a large town. She sat in a rocking chair on that porch.

Dawson turned to look at the woman sitting next to her. She had never been tall, but was even more shortened with age. Her white hair was short, her skin thin and white as new parchment. She sat with a blanket over her lap, and a cup of tea steaming on the table between them.

The aged figure turned to her, and Dawson was transfixed by her eyes. Those dark brown eyes were the eyes of a person used to command, to the wielding of tremendous authority. With a shock, in the old woman's features Dawson recognized her own, the family resemblance clear.

"Hello, grandchild. I am Jan Childers.

"That you are seeing this recording means that you are the next person in the chain of Watchers, intended to keep an eye on Galactic Mail. I cannot know how many years have passed by now, or which generation you are. I cannot answer your questions, but I can probably anticipate many of them. It is for that purpose this recording is being made.

"When we created Galactic Mail – Bill Campbell, Jake Turner, Miriam Desai, myself, and others – we bound it with all the legal and administrative chains we could to keep it from morphing into a government. Yet we expect such chains will thin and weaken under the constant pull exerted on them. It is for this reason we put in place another mechanism to restrain Galactic Mail. Twenty-four chains of our descendants, who have extraordinary access into the systems on which Galactic Mail depends, and who can reset the organization to its original, limited purpose.

"You are the newest member of this group, and this is your initial briefing on your position, your powers, and your responsibilities.

"We set up Galactic Mail to solve a single problem, the predation of one star system upon another, throughout all of human space. To put a stop to interstellar war, permanently. An ambitious goal, to be sure. Yet, as I sit here talking to you, it has held now for over fifty years.

"That is a tremendous achievement by itself. In the thirty years I served in the Commonwealth Space Force, we fought no fewer than two major wars and literally hundreds of incursions. While the CSF was largely successful in repelling such incursions, among the Outer Colonies, the number of incursions was much larger. The death toll of all these incursions is impossible to know, but surely ran into the tens of millions. The human toll of the destruction of infrastructure in poverty, disease, and misery can only be guessed at.

"That was in a mere thirty years. Yet, in the fifty-some years since we started Galactic Mail, there have been no successful incursions, by anyone, anywhere. In truth, there have been very few attempts, given that the existence of Galactic Mail doomed them to failure. By now, most star systems have forsaken the study and practice of interstellar war, and, having seen more than my share, I can say that has been a very good thing.

"And I would like to keep it going."

Childers picked up her tea and sipped it, while looking out at the New Hope of her time. When she had collected her thoughts, she set the tea down, turned back to Patricia Dawson, and continued.

"There are two primary dangers to Galactic Mail. One is external, that some system will stumble upon some new military technology that would make Galactic Mail vulnerable to being countered and allow that system to take up war on its neighbors with impunity. We have taken steps to forestall that eventuality, by instituting research within Galactic Mail to continue to sharpen its technology over time. We hope that, with the resources it has available, it can maintain its lead for quite a while. The estimates put it quite a few hundred years into the future, assuming Galactic Mail maintains its research posture and doesn't dissipate its resources on other adventures.

"The second danger is internal, that, having achieved its purpose, Galactic Mail will look for new problems to solve, other activities it can undertake to better the human condition. This is a great danger. Allow me to explain why.

"Human beings are messy creatures. We have all sorts of impulses and desires and motives, not all of them noble or honorable or benign. Anything but. That is the human condition. It is not solvable. We set out with Galactic Mail to close off the one worst aberrant behavior of the human race, death and destruction on a massive scale, through war on our fellow man. To have achieved that, to the extent we have, is remarkable.

"But the temptation will exist to solve other problems. In the end, to solve all other problems. This will arise from the noblest of motives, but it is wrong-headed, for two reasons.

"The first is that, in doing so, Galactic Mail will take its eye off the ball, dissipate its energies, will not remain adept and skilled at its primary purpose, maintaining a moratorium on war. War is the great leveler, it tears down everything, reduces humanity to its most basic impulses, and opens the door to every possible evil. Famine, plague, genocide, and worse. Take it from a lifelong student of war, that the abolition of war is the one great accomplishment. All others are secondary.

"The second reason is more subtle. While our basic humanity aches to help the poor, the hungry, the ill, the oppressed, when such efforts are centralized, a great truth emerges. Altruism doesn't scale well. In fact, such efforts usually end very badly. Dependence destroys independence. It is such a truth that it is built into the language.

"For these reasons, in our effort to rid humanity of the one great evil of war, we left many smaller evils alone. Over time, many of these smaller evils will be solved on a smaller scale, once the disruption of war is removed. The great tyrannies often resulted from the dislocations of war. Without the presence of war, over time they dissipate. That is our belief and our hope.

"But it is a slow process. The temptation will naturally arise within Galactic Mail to solve such problems more quickly, to step into the internal politics of star systems, ultimately to use its tremendous military power to force its solutions on individual star systems.

"What one ends up with then is a galactic central government.

"Uniting all of humanity under one government would be a tremendous mistake. Sooner or later, even the most benevolent and well-intentioned government can be corrupted, turn to despotism. To where, then, would one flee to escape it? From what outside point could one oppose it? Humanity would sink into millennia of tyranny.

"We decided the possibility – more, the likelihood – of tyranny on individual planets was a lesser evil than tyranny on the grand scale, across all of humanity. Galactic Mail is structured to prevent a galactic government from forming, as long as it does not become one itself.

"But we believe it will, or at least it will try.

"It is for this reason that you watch. It is your great responsibility."

Dawson paused the recording. She looked out over the older version of New Hope absently.

Sitting here on this porch with her tea and her blanket, almost a hundred years old, and looking out over the small town New Hope was at the time, Grandma Childers spoke of these huge issues – galactic issues – so matter-of-factly. While heading up a navy of millions of people protecting thirty-three star systems, she herself had created Galactic Mail even while expecting it to try to become a galactic government.

She had understood that Galactic Mail would try to become a government for all the best of reasons. To take on other human issues, solve other human problems, setting the stage for tyranny by trying to be all things to all people, the solution to every ill.

She had spoken just as matter-of-factly about two dozen people taking it over, reconstituting it around its core mission. The most powerful organization humanity had ever created, ensuring the peace among what were now tens of thousands of inhabited planets. Against all this she ranged two-dozen people.

Dawson thought about that little old lady, the changes she had wrought, how they echoed across the years, the centuries, and how she had seen the future, and prepared against it. Dawson felt suddenly inadequate to the task.

My God. What have I gotten myself in for? she thought.

Allies

Dawson checked the time in the VR control panel. She still had time to get down to the gym for her workout before the kids got home. She stopped the simulation and was back in reality, in her office, in their home in suburban New Hope. She headed for the bedroom, shedding her clothes on the way.

As she dressed in her gym clothes, she continued to ponder the vast forces at work in the world around her, unseen and, before her assignment as a Watcher, unknown. Grandma Lieber had carried this burden for seventy years. No wonder she had sighed when Dawson sent the mail.

As she was doing her warm-up stretches, she saw George Enfield sparring Enshin on the mats. They were wearing helmets, and pulling their punches. Enshin karate was a full-contact style, but not for sparring. Half judo and half karate, Enshin was popular on Horizon, likely because it had been popular in the Commonwealth Space Force, and a lot of CSF people had retired here, either at the time of Horizon's founding or after.

Enfield looked to be about ten years older than her, in his late thirties. Dawson knew he was a distant cousin, in the family line of Margaret Childers Campbell, Jan Childers' other child. Dawson had never sparred with George, but they knew each other a bit from seeing each other at the gym. Now, though, a thought struck her.

As Enfield came by on the way to the water fountain, Dawson struck up a conversation.

"Hi, George."

"Oh, hi, Patty."

"George, you're my nth-cousin or something, aren't you?"

"I think so," George said. "My seventh great grandparents were Jan Childers and Bill Campbell."

"Mine, too. That would make us what? Like eighth cousins or something?"

"That sounds right."

"And we're both into Enshin. Isn't that weird?" Dawson asked.

"My great grandfather encouraged me to take it up when I was a teenager. I really enjoyed it, so I stayed at it."

"My great grandmother encouraged me as well. What else do you like? What are your other hobbies?"

"Well, I like the shooting sports. Hunting in the hills east of New Hope. Target shooting. Some tactical shooting, even. And I like strategy games. There's some really good ones in VR," Enfield said.

"And your great grandfather encouraged you in those, too, right?"

"Yes, actually."

"Just like my great grandmother," Dawson said. "How strange. I guess as family traditions go, this must be a Childers one."

She inflected it as 'Childers 1' and Enfield started a bit. His eyes narrowed, but he went on normally.

"Well, you're a Childers, too."

Ha! He said it as 'Childers 2.'

"Why, yes. Yes, I am."

After that, Enfield and Dawson started training together. When they sparred at Enshin, she, ten years younger, was faster, but he, ten years more experienced, was more cunning.

They started shooting together as well. Dawson enrolled in a tactical shooting course Enfield recommended, then took two follow-on courses. She was already an accomplished target shooter, and she took to the tactical shooting well.

They began hunting together, in the hills east of town, up behind Campbell Hall. They had both been hunters before, but they found the companionship comfortable, and enjoyed hunting trips together more than either had alone.

Dawson also viewed the rest of the VR through to the end. The plans, the decision points, the branches. She realized she was seeing the end result of thousands of staff hours of preparation and planning, for a confrontation they earnestly hoped would not happen, but were all too confident would come about eventually.

There were more VR training materials available on request. She requested them all and began training in earnest. As the role of Watcher came with a substantial stipend, siphoned off by the computers from some account in the vast cash-flow that was Galactic Mail, Dawson could quit her job and devote her efforts full-time to training and simulations.

She realized from the start these training classes and simulations were not from the time of Jan Childers. They were current Galactic Mail training classes and simulations from the Galactic Mail Academy, which taught the officers and ship captains who served in Galactic Mail. She exercised in simulations with current Galactic Mail hardware. She studied the strategies and tactics of Galactic Mail.

She also studied strategy and tactics from multiple other sources, everything from the ancient texts of Sun Tzu and Clausewitz through *The Science of Surprise* by Jan Childers.

How to handle all this with Bob Morgan, her husband, bothered Dawson for quite a while. Did she tell him? Could she tell him? How could she *not* tell him?

Ultimately she decided to just ask him.

One night after the kids were in bed, she sat down with him at the kitchen table.

"I have something extremely confidential I don't know whether to tell you about or not," Dawson said.

"How confidential?" Morgan asked. He was an attorney, who often handled confidential matters for clients. Confidentiality was something he understood.

"If I thought it was going to come out, and my death would prevent it, I would kill myself to keep it a secret."

"Truly?" Morgan asked.

"Truly. No question at all."

"Then don't tell me. Don't tell anybody. Does anyone else know?"

"My distant cousin George Enfield knows. That's it." *Well, on Horizon, anyway*, Dawson thought.

"Is it illegal?" Morgan asked.

"No."

"Is it dangerous?"

"Not yet. It could become so, but the odds are against it," Dawson said.

"Is there anything I absolutely need to know about it?"

"It's in the nature of a job. A position, really. It pays a hefty stipend. That you need to know, because we're going to have more money coming in. It will involve me full-time, with a lot of VR work. So I need to quit my job to do this so I can work at home during the day. And George is in on it, so he and I will be spending a good deal of time together. That's it."

"And you're sure it's not illegal," Morgan said.

"Absolutely." *The current leadership of Galactic Mail may not like it if they found out about it, but Galactic Mail doesn't have the status of a government, and so it can't make things illegal*, Dawson thought. *That's the whole point.*

"Well, I'm curious as hell about it, but if it's as confidential and important as you say, I would really rather not know. And I'll cover for you."

"Thanks, Hon. I appreciate it."

Morgan was as good as his word. He called it her new job. When anyone asked him about it, he just said, "Hey, she's an accountant. She tried to tell me about it, and I fell asleep in about ten seconds. Really, whenever I'm having trouble falling asleep, I ask her about her job. Works every time."

Training

After Dawson quit her job, she kicked her training into high gear. She immersed herself in the Academy's training classes, working her way through the entire curriculum, then the graduate tactical classes, the leadership classes, and the management classes.

She took multiple tactical shooting classes, until the gun was an extension of herself, as natural in her hand as her hand being empty. At the urging of her instructors, she worked on being smooth, not fast.

"When you master smooth, you will become fast."

She dry-fired a thousand times a week, until she finally conquered her flinch, and her patterns tightened up dramatically.

Early on, she asked the computer if she could obtain supplies through Galactic Mail, and the computer responded in the affirmative. She asked George and her tactical shooting instructors what were the best weapons, holster rigs, and ammunition to use in a real gunfight, cost be damned, and ordered twenty of the guns, a dozen holster rigs, and ten thousand rounds of ammunition through Galactic Mail. She got a recommendation for a gunsmith, and had him personally go through each weapon and tweak them for combat, rejecting any that fell short of his most exacting standards.

About a year into her training, Dawson and Enfield were cooling down after an Enshin bout, in a corner of the gym where they couldn't be overheard.

"Anything else I should be doing, George?" Dawson asked.

"Well, I'd like you to copy me on your training program. I want to make sure I haven't missed anything."

"Sure, I can do that."

"Thanks," Enfield said. "You know, I wonder. I know we can't know who the other Watchers are, or send them messages to try to influence their voting – you know, talk them into a decision they don't come to on their own – but I wonder if we can send them your training program. Someone who is out there by themselves with this responsibility may not know what to do to be prepared. We could give them some guidance if we could send them your training program."

"I'll ask. Anything else?"

"Yes. Get a voice coach. Move your voice range down an octave, and work on your command voice. Seriously work on it. I think you're going to need it."

Dawson checked with the computers. Yes, she could anonymously send materials to all the Watchers, as long as she stayed away from advocacy touching on their decision-making responsibility. She prepared her training program, and sent it on to Galactic Mail as the recommended training program for Watchers.

She also had the computer notify all the Watchers of the availability of obtaining weapons and other supplies through Galactic Mail. She included her weapon, rig, and ammo choices in her training program recommendation.

She noted that all Galactic Mail's press releases, as well as their in-house clipping service, were accessible to all Watchers. She asked the computers to change that from just access to actually sending them out to all Watchers in real time, and the computers agreed and complied.

From then on, she and all the Watchers received a news feed on Galactic Mail.

Dawson followed Enfield's advice to work with a voice coach. She was worried about what Morgan would think when she began speaking an octave lower, but he said he found it sexy. That increased her motivation, and her progress was good.

She also found command voice worked remarkably well on the children.

Dawson settled into a new routine, training in earnest full-time. Enshin, shooting, strategy, leadership. Five years passed, and she began to hope her new and hard-earned skills would be unneeded, that her time on watch would pass without those skills being tested.

It was not to be.

Frustration and Triumph

"Did you see this?" Padma Kosar tossed a printout on Sylvain Costa's desk and flopped in one of his guest chairs. It was early morning at Galactic Mail's headquarters on Doma, and the sun was only about an hour above the mountains to the east.

Costa looked at it and sighed.

"Yes. There's still nothing I can do about it, Padma."

"You're the CEO of Galactic Mail. What do you mean you can't do anything about it?"

Costa looked at his chief of staff sympathetically.

"Look, I agree with you. I'd like to clean some of these bastards out once and for all. But I don't yet have a majority behind me on the Board. If I tried now, I would likely be removed. And then you and I end up honored retirees, and nothing gets done."

He picked up the printout and scanned it. The casualty numbers had been updated since last night. The Grand Duke of the planet Wallachia had put down a rebellion with a kinetic orbital bombardment of the rebel forces, which were holed up in two cities. The total dead and missing was now figured to be on the order of three hundred and fifty thousand men, women, and children.

It hadn't even made the list of top stories in today's news. With thirty-five thousand planets, the terrors that were regularly inflicted on the populations of a thousand or so of them were old news, and didn't affect most people's lives much. While ninety-eight percent of humanity went about its business, two percent or so lived under absolute tyranny.

And Costa couldn't change that. Yet.

"One more Board election and we should have it, Padma. Of the eight Board members retiring next election, six of them are against me on this. If we get even three more Board members that agree with me, we could do something about this crap."

"So we need five total of the eight incoming?"

"Yeah, that would do it, with a spare or two. I already have five of the other eight. But I can't get out on a limb on this. If I were to act

19

now, and lose a Board motion on a nine-to-seven vote – which is what it would be, let me assure you – then I'm out. And our chance to reinterpret Galactic Mail's charter to keep this sort of thing from happening into the future goes right out the window."

"And if you were removed instead, that would set back progress substantially."

"Absolutely. I'm three years into my second term, and I'm pretty popular with the Board and the employees. And we've been gradually winning the Board over to our point of view over the last ten or twelve years. But I still don't have a majority. If I were to be removed by the Board for acting on this –" he waved the printout in his hand "– it would tell every CEO of Galactic Mail for the next fifty years they shouldn't go down this path, and the tyrants and dictators would breathe easy. We might lose our chance to stop this terror forever.

"Look, the next Board meeting is in two years. What we need to do is work up some solid candidates for the Board who share our thinking. Half the planets don't even send delegates to the shareholders meetings anymore. If we can get some proxies, and subtly push some candidates over others, we should be able to get the three more votes we need."

"OK, OK. It just galls the hell out of me these bastards pull this crap, and we have all this technology and military power, and we don't do anything about it."

"Oh, I understand, Padma. Trust me, I understand. And I agree with you. But we need to take this a step at a time to get it done. In the meantime, things are going to have to go on as they are a while longer. Let's get working on identifying some solid Board candidates for that next election. It's not too soon to start.

"The other thing we can do is start a little list. Let's put the Grand Duke of Wallachia at the top of it."

"We have a little over ten thousand proxies out of a hundred and five thousand or so shares," Kosar said.

"Excellent, Padma," Costa said. "Excellent. And with fifty thousand or so attending, an additional ten thousand votes we can cast for our candidates is a big help. We should be able to get the five candidates we need. At least. And how's our list coming?"

"Our top tier, our Most Not Wanted list, is twenty planets."

"Soon, then. We will likely be able to act on them soon."

The Galactic Mail shareholders meeting was held in an arena built for the purpose in a natural bowl in the hills between Galactic Mail's headquarters site and the city of Nadezhda on Doma. The arena was used for other purposes by both Galactic Mail and Nadezhda, and had rail service from both the Galactic Mail headquarters and the Nadezhda municipal transit systems.

With fifty thousand shareholders attending, three from each of the planets who had sent delegates, the process for nominating members of the Board of Directors was largely held in advance of the meeting, via mail. Last minute nominations were admitted at the shareholders meeting, and the short speeches by all the candidates lasted a total of three days.

In the end, the ten thousand proxies proved decisive. The candidates whom management supported took six of the eight open seats on the Board.

After fifteen years as CEO of Galactic Mail, Sylvain Costa finally had the majority he wanted.

Decision and Action

"I don't like this plan," said John Meisner, a Board member of Galactic Mail, to the rest of the Board. "I think it deviates too strongly from what has been for one hundred and seventy-five years a working strategy. I've circulated around to you all some of the published discussion that occurred among the founders of Galactic Mail. It is clear their greatest worry was that Galactic Mail would morph into a galactic central government. I think this is too much of a step in that direction, and I recommend against it."

"Galactic Mail is not a central government, John, and this change will not make it one," Koit Strnad said.

"Military action in response to events internal to a system? How is that not the sort of action a central government takes? It presumes the authority to judge a planetary government's actions, and thereby makes Galactic Mail superior to the planetary government," Meisner said.

"Galactic Mail has always been there to defend planets against space-based attack. This is a minor change, in which Galactic Mail will prevent the planet from a space-based attack by its own government. I really don't see what the big problem is," said Humaira Zhao.

"That's a bit of a sleight of hand, Humaira," Donal Suzuki said. "The mission of Galactic Mail has always been to protect *systems* from space-based attack by *other* systems. Interplanetary attack. Not internal matters within a star system."

Zhao waved her hand. "As I say, a slight change. I have no problem with it. I do have a problem with the sort of thing we see going on, in which governments bombard their own people. That is what I am opposed to. I am surprised you are not."

The excitable Suzuki was about to jump out of his seat, but a hand on his arm from Meisner restrained him.

"Of course, we're opposed to the orbital bombardment of people by their own government," Meisner said. "The question before us today is whether it is Galactic Mail's responsibility to prevent or punish it.

As I've said before, there is a danger there. One that our founders saw clearly. It is too bad we have lost that clarity of vision in the one hundred and seventy-five years since."

Zhao took a breath to continue the volley, but Strnad cut her off.

"Further discussion will get us nowhere. I call the vote."

"Very well," Chairman of the Board Maxwell Guerrero said. "By show of hands. All in favor? All opposed? Let the record show the Ayes have it, by a vote of eleven to five.

"May God have mercy on us all," Suzuki said.

"OK, so the Board passed the resolution. Do we get to hammer these guys now?" Kosar asked.

"No, Padma. What we do is hit them if they do it again, on a going forward basis," Costa said.

"So they get away with what they did?"

"I didn't say that. We wait. If they do it again, then we check whether it's the first time or not. Whether they're on our list or not."

"And if it's not their first time?"

"Then we hit them hard."

Word of Galactic Mail's new policy went out to all human planets. Most people who paid any attention to it at all regarded it as a good thing. Some thought it was well past due. A few planetary governments, not by any means tyrannies, had grave misgivings, but they were in the minority.

The word also got out to the resistance movements on various planets. Knowing Galactic Mail would intervene in the case of kinetic bombardment emboldened them to act now, before Galactic Mail changed its mind.

Over the next three months, revolutionary movements stepped up their attacks on their local governments on hundreds of planets. In twenty-three of these, the hard-pressed governments responded with kinetic attacks from space.

Galactic Mail responded.

Two hunting parties of beam weapon drones and a nuclear weapon drone dropped out of hyperspace in the Algused system. They accelerated toward the planet. As the drones swept past the planet, the hunter/killers targeted all the police enforcement ships in space. The single nuclear weapon drone targeted the large space station the police maintained to service their orbital ships, and its ten megaton warhead vaporized the station.

Their job done, the drones returned to Doma.

"Well, we're making a difference now, at least. These little tin-pot dictators know they can't bombard their own citizens with impunity," Kosar said.

"How many is that now?" Costa asked.

"Twenty-three."

"And we've limited our strikes to space-based police infrastructure?"

"Yes, sir. Although I think that's a mistake."

"I know you do, Padma. But for a first-time offender, that's as far as I'm willing to go right now."

Costa's terminal sounded a priority warning. He turned to it, and his eyebrows went up as he read.

"Another kinetic strike?" Kosar asked.

"Yes. On Wallachia."

"Yes! We're finally going to get that bastard. I've been hoping for this."

Costa found Kosar's glee at this development more than a little disturbing.

"You sound happy he bombarded his own planet."

"Not at all. But I am happy that, at least in this case, we get to take the gloves off. Orders, sir?"

Costa sighed. The moment of decision had arrived.

"Attack Plan Alpha."

Twenty-seven drones dropped out of hyperspace in the Wallachia system and accelerated towards the planet. As the drones swept past the planet, the hunter/killers targeted all the police enforcement ships in space. A nuclear weapon drone targeted the large space station the police maintained to service their orbital ships, and its ten megaton warhead vaporized the station.

Additionally, kinetic strike drones hit the Grand Duke's palace and his summer home, the House of Lords, and the headquarters of the security services in the capital. Two nuclear weapons hit the two large police bases, one on each major continent, which were located away from the cities to protect them from their own citizenry.

Having wiped out the police forces and decapitated the regime, the drones returned to Doma.

Hesitation and Resolve

"Did you see the announcement by Galactic Mail about the ban on kinetic orbital strikes?" Enfield asked.

"Yes. I saw that, then requested the private minutes of the Board meeting where they passed a resolution 'reinterpreting' the charter. I put those minutes in the distribution to the Watchers."

"Ah. So that was you."

They were walking in the woods above Campbell Hall, where they couldn't be overheard or monitored.

"Yes, it was me," Dawson said. "I also went back and looked at the vote tallies of the shareholders meeting. Only half the shareholders attended, and management voted ten thousand proxies."

"Ouch. That's a hole in the structure Jan Childers didn't see."

"I don't think it ever occurred to her a planet wouldn't bother sending delegates to the shareholders meeting. Or that management would solicit proxies."

"That was a failure of imagination. Voter participation in democracies falls when people are happy. They get complacent. Well documented in Earth history," Enfield said.

"And now the Board has voted to abandon the charter. Or rather, 'reinterpret' the charter."

"Same difference. What it means is Galactic Mail is officially off the rails. So do we vote to take it over now?"

"I don't think so," Dawson said. "When and if we take it over, there is going to be a lot of breakage. People dead, stuff blown up, our existence revealed. It's going to be a messy process. We only have one shot at this."

"You don't think it's time yet, then?"

"Not yet."

"So I guess we get to wait and see where this goes," Enfield said.

"Yeah. But you're right. I sure don't like the look of where it's headed."

Another day, another walk in the woods.

"How many is that now?" Enfield asked.

"How many what?" Dawson asked.

"How many systems where Galactic Mail acted outside what it's charter was always understood to allow?"

"Twenty-one systems."

"So far," Enfield said.

"Yeah. Twenty-one so far. But in none of these has Galactic Mail hit anything other than space-based resources of the system police forces. No planet hits, no civilian damage. They just hit the regime security forces, and only in space."

"So you don't think it's time yet."

"No. Not yet. Maybe this is as far as they'll go," Dawson said.

"All right. I'll go along with you. But I don't think they're going to stop here."

"I don't either, but I hope they do."

Several weeks later, Dawson was much more somber during their walk.

"Galactic Mail hit Wallachia. Decapitated the regime, multiple planetary hits, nuclear weapons on the planet's surface. The whole nine yards," Dawson said.

"Yeah, they bombarded the planet to punish the regime for bombarding the planet. You have to appreciate the irony there," Enfield said.

"No, I don't. I don't appreciate it at all. It means I have to set aside the life I've lived, the things I love, and go off to war because they're too damned stupid to leave a good thing well enough alone."

"So it's time?"

"Yes, it's time. And I already made sure all the news clippings and Galactic Mail press releases were still in the distribution list. We'll see if a majority agrees. But I'm going to vote to take over Galactic Mail," Dawson said.

"Well, I'm with you, Pat. I'm going to send my vote in as well. And, whatever happens, I'll be there with you."

"I appreciate it, George. I really do."

Back at home, Dawson stared at the words on her screen. Jan Childers must have been psychic. Vision alone couldn't account for it, for how clearly she had seen the stark choices, the terrible burden, that would face her descendants. How well those words encapsulated Dawson's current position. It was her right. It was her duty.

Whatever else happened, her life would never be the same.

She read them again, sighed, and hit Send.

"... it is their right, it is their duty, to throw off such Government, and to provide new Guards for their future security."

Notification

Two days later, Dawson received by mail the official notification the Watchers had voted in the majority to overturn the management of Galactic Mail and take over the corporation. A Galactic Mail ship would be arriving to take them on board in about two weeks.

That night, with the kids in bed, they were sitting at the kitchen table.

"You know how I said the odds were against this confidential project becoming dangerous?" Dawson asked.

"Yes," Morgan said.

"Well, it just became dangerous."

Dawson told him the whole story: her recruitment by her great grandmother, Grandma Lieber; the line of Watchers, keeping tabs on Galactic Mail, guarding against its transition to a galactic government; her intuition that George Enfield was the other Childers Watcher, and confirming it that day at the gym; her training efforts, both separately and together with Enfield; their sending their vote that Galactic Mail had gone off the rails; and the notice she had just received that a majority of the Watchers agreed.

"That's an amazing story. This introduction by Jan Childers. Can I VR that?"

"Sure."

Dawson didn't keep any materials related to her role as a Watcher on her system. She handed him the memory chip and he went back into his home office to view it. He was a while returning.

"Sorry about that. I checked out the language in the incorporation papers while I was there. They had some pretty good lawyers draw up those documents. The authority for the Watchers is in there, but it doesn't jump out at you," Morgan said.

"I looked for it and didn't find it."

"'The Board may be removed at any time by a one-quarter vote of the shareholders, or by a majority vote of such other group as may be established by the Board, and a new Board elected by the shareholders or by such other group.' Welcome to 'such other group.'"

"Ah, that's it. The Board must have passed a measure to establish the Watchers at some point, and it's buried in mountains of Board measures passed over the decades since," Dawson said.

"Yep. So the authority is there, built into the initial incorporation papers, in the non-amendable portion of Galactic Mail's charter."

"So Jan Childers saw the need for such a group before Galactic Mail was even founded."

"She had to have. It was in the initial filing," Morgan said.

"Amazing."

"I'll say. And that introduction by her was remarkable."

"In what way?" Dawson asked.

"In a whole bunch of ways. Mostly her vision. That she could see all this coming. That she could plan against it, almost two centuries in advance. Ninety-some years old, sitting in a rocking chair sipping her tea, on a colony planet, looking out over the sleepy little town New Hope was at that time, and planning and steering the future of the galaxy hundreds of years in advance. And her personal power. The VR fairly vibrated with her authority. Remarkable." Morgan looked up at Dawson, scanned her face. "You look a lot like her, you know."

"I noticed that. But I'm descended from her along three different lines. It was a small colony, after all, and I'm eight generations removed from her. But it looks like some of those crossbreeds reinforced," Dawson said.

"I suspect you're right, because your resemblance to her is clear, other than your height."

"But that wasn't genetic with her. That was malnourishment during her growth years. I wonder how tall she would have been if not for that."

"No way of knowing."

Dawson and Enfield met once more in the woods at their favorite hunting blind, in the hills above Campbell Hall.

"We must have been the votes that put us over the top," Dawson said.

"Not necessarily. It could have been the same news report that triggered a lot of votes. But, either way, we're in it now," Enfield said.

"I guess it's time to review the procedures and plans again. I wonder just how difficult this is going to be."

"It's not going to be easy. The people who run the joint aren't going to want to just give up and walk away. And don't forget, they think they're the good guys."

"And we're on the side of the tyrants. Yes, I know," Dawson said

"They're going to fight us. They're going to pull out all the stops. And so, Patricia Dawson, I have a question for you. Just how ruthless are you willing to be?"

"I've been giving that a lot of thought. I'm only an accountant, but I'm good with numbers. There are approximately four trillion human beings in the galaxy right now, on thirty-five thousand planets. That will grow fast. Jan Childers said she expected a galactic tyranny to last millenia. Call it a hundred generations. We're looking at a tyranny over literally quadrillions of human lives. I guess whether we have to kill a few hundred, or a few thousand, or even a few million, we're still way ahead. It would even make sense to destroy a whole planet – killing billions – if we had to.

"What we can't afford to do is fail."

"OK," Enfield said. "I wanted to make sure you thought all that through, because I think that's the right answer. But that means things could get very messy indeed. We can't afford to lose, even once. If we have to kill millions to preserve the Watchers, to continue against Galactic Mail, we have to be prepared to do that. If we have to tear the whole organization down, kill everyone in it, and let all the planets go back to squabbling and interplanetary war, even that would be preferable to a galactic government. I just wanted to make sure you knew that."

"I do. Damn. This isn't going to be at all pleasant, is it?"

"I suspect not."

Dawson looked vacantly out at the woods and sighed. "Well, it will be what it will be." She turned back to Enfield. "I guess I'll see you at the spaceport in a week or so. Are you bringing Tatiana?"

"Yes, I think so. She's got a good head on her shoulders and is a fair shot. What about you? Are you bringing Rob?"

"Yes. You never can tell when you're going to need a good lawyer," Dawson said.

"And the kids?"

"I think it's time for a vacation with Grandma at Campbell Hall. What about you?"

"Our youngest just started college. They'll stay here," Morgan said.

"All right. See you next week. Be in touch if you think of anything we should talk about in the meantime."

"You, too. See ya."

GMS *Mnemosyne*

"Secure from hyperspace. Set course for the planet. One-g acceleration," said Captain Gregory Bowers, captain of the GMS *Mnemosyne*.

"Securing from hyperspace, Sir. Setting course for the planet, one-g acceleration."

Captain Bowers considered his orders. He had been told nothing more than to pick up VIP passengers on various planets scattered throughout human space, primarily in what was considered The Old Sector of the galaxy, the ancient and populous planets clustering around Earth. He was not given a final destination for these passengers. The last two, here on Horizon, would leave him in orbit with eighteen VIP passengers and their families, and no word yet on where to take them. Damn curious.

Dispatching a ship as large as *Mnemosyne* to such a task was ludicrous on its face. *Mnemosyne* was a passenger liner that could accommodate ten thousand passengers in individual first-class accommodations, one of a dozen such huge ships used to transport shareholders to the quinquennial shareholders meeting. With thirty-five thousand human planets, the one hundred and five thousand shareholders – or what portion of them chose to attend – were brought in to twelve regional centers, from which the Titan ships would transport them to the shareholders meeting on Doma, the home planet of Galactic Mail. Using such a ship to pick up eighteen passengers and their families? Curiouser still.

The passengers were a mixed bag, ranging from their mid-twenties to their eighties or beyond. Most brought their spouses with them, and sometimes minor children. Most had never traveled in space before. When they came aboard the ship, they looked around curiously, and had to be instructed in the very basics of space travel. Weightlessness pills, strapping in under maneuvering, all that sort of thing. And yet, they came aboard with a weird sort of possessiveness, like the ship was theirs, and they had just never gotten around to checking it out before. Curiouser and curiouser.

Still, orders is orders. No doubt the powers that be would let him know what to do next when they got around to it.

What Bowers did not know was those orders had been cut by a computer without any human intervention or motivation. *Mnemosyne* was currently running off the books.

"You kids behave for Grandma, all right? I don't want any bad reports when I get back."

"We will, Mom," both Jenny and Billy replied as they each gave her a hug and a kiss goodbye.

"They'll be fine, Pat. They're never any trouble."

"All right, Mom. Thanks again, and on such short notice."

"You just go and do what you need to do, Honey. And good luck."

Dawson gave her mother a sharp look. Her mom held up her hand with the thumb and forefinger held about a quarter-inch apart.

"Just this much, from my grandmother. That the chain be unbroken if something untimely happened to her. You run along now. We'll be fine."

Her mother gave her a hug, like a normal goodbye, but there was a tear in her eye. Like she knew this could be the last time.

Dawson gave her an extra squeeze, then she and Bob got back in the ground car and headed for the spaceport.

The New Hope Spaceport was primarily a freight operation. Inbound and outbound freight, as well as refueling and resupply for Galactic Mail ships calling at New Hope, were the primary activities. The passenger terminal was a single building, with half a dozen shuttle landing pads.

Morgan and Dawson met up with George Enfield and his wife, Tatiana Khatri, at the spaceport. They waited together for the shuttle from GMS *Mnemosyne* to arrive.

Dawson and Enfield knew something most people didn't. While *Mnemosyne* was a large passenger liner, it was also, like all Galactic Mail ships, a drone tender. That is, a warship. Its normal complement was six hunting parties and four additional sensor/courier drones. Each hunting party was nine beam weapon drones and a sensor/command drone. So *Mnemosyne* came into Horizon with sixty-four drone companions. Likely they were all in hyperspace save two, which would be sitting outside the hyperspace-1 limit, where they could drop into hyperspace and signal other drones to respond.

That *Mnemosyne* was a warship figured into their plans.

The shuttle dropped to the landing pad while they watched. Once it had spooled down, crew members in Galactic Mail passenger crew livery emerged and stowed their luggage aboard the shuttle while others welcomed them into its passenger space.

It was a large passenger shuttle, and seated two hundred. In the vestibule, a security team waited to scan and search them on boarding. Dawson stopped before the security team and held up a hand.

"*Mnemosyne* computer. Dawson here."

After a slight delay for the transmission to orbit and back, the response came.

"Yes, Ms. Dawson."

"Is it policy to search Galactic Mail VIP guests when boarding?"

"No, Ms. Dawson."

"Does this security team have the captain's written orders to search us in violation of Galactic Mail standard policy?"

"No, Ms. Dawson."

Dawson told the security team, "I refuse your voluntary search process, thank you," and stepped past them, and around the scanner, into the cabin.

The shuttle crew was a bit nonplussed, but let her by. Morgan, Enfield, and Khatri followed.

Dawson had one more comment for the crew.

"That goes for our luggage as well."

All four passengers were offered and took anti-weightlessness-sickness pills. Then the shuttle pilot spooled up the engines and lifted for orbit. Dawson watched out the window as the shuttle lifted. She had never been in space before, and it was interesting to see New Hope from above as they lifted.

The shuttle flight took about forty-five minutes. *Mnemosyne* was on her side of the shuttle as they docked. It was a huge ship, with ten large cabin cylinders folded out from the central structure as she rotated to provide apparent gravity in her personnel spaces. She looked like a huge daisy spinning in space. Her long axis lie along a radius from the planet, her aft drive engines pointed toward the surface and her bows pointed out into space.

The shuttle bay was one of a set of racks on the bow of the ship, in the center of multiple rows of reaction mass and supply containers ringing the front portion of the ship, forward of the cabin cylinders. The shuttle racks were arranged around the front hyperspace projector, which looked like a small version of the aft drive engines. Five other shuttles occupied the racks, leaving one open for them to dock to. The front bulkhead with the racks was being counter-rotated with respect to the ship so the racks were stationary for docking.

Once they were docked, the bulkhead was spun up to match the rotation of the ship and latched into place. Boarding tubes extended from the ship's bow the few feet to the hatches of the shuttle.

Once the boarding tubes were in place, the crew invited them to debark the shuttle in the near-zero gravity, and stood by to assist them through the boarding tube and to the stairs down into the ship.

Both Dawson and Enfield were wearing high turtleneck sweaters, not unusual in early fall on Horizon. They had the added benefit of covering the VR remote they each wore on the back of their neck at the base of the skull. Dawson had requested the expensive units sent out to all eighteen new Board members when the notification came, and they had shipped out via Galactic Mail Express Service, beating the *Mnemosyne* to their recipients.

When Dawson passed into the ship, she VRed the ship's computer and presented her digital identification, including various command codes she had received from Galactic Mail's central computer systems. She got the acknowledgement back over the VR, and relaxed. That was one thing she had been worried about.

Her captain and crew didn't know it yet, but *Mnemosyne* was hers.

In the circular corridor that joined the top of the ten cylinders, crewmen were moving their luggage in the 0.1-g gravity this close to the axis of the ship. Other crewmen were motioning them towards the hatch to the ladderway to cylinder four, while the porters with their luggage were heading toward the ladderway to cylinder two.

"Baggage detail, halt!" Dawson said in her command voice. She had been practicing with a voice coach for years, and could produce a command voice one did not want to disobey.

The crewmen halted. Dawson walked around in front of them.

"Just where are you going with our luggage?" Dawson asked.

"Uh, to Ship Security, Ma'am."

"Computer, is it Galactic Mail standard procedure to search the luggage of VIP passenger guests."

"No, Ms. Dawson."

"Does the security team have the captain's written orders to search our luggage, overriding Galactic Mail standard policy?"

"No, Ms. Dawson."

"What is the Galactic Mail standard policy for luggage of VIP passenger guests?"

"The baggage is to be transferred directly to the VIP passenger guest's cabin per Galactic Mail standard policy."

"But we have our orders, Ma'am," the senior porter of the detail said.

"Yes, you do. Galactic Mail standard policy here constitutes your orders. Per that policy, any other orders you have received without the captain's written override are without authority. I suppose we could just comm Captain Bowers directly and have him resolve this if you have a problem following Galactic Mail standard policy. I'm not sure he'd like to be interrupted from whatever he's doing at the moment to explain standard policy to you, but if you want to do that, I have no problem with it."

"Uh, no, Ma'am. That would not be my first choice."

"OK, good. Look. You almost screwed up, big time, but I'll let it go for now. Come on, let's go. To our cabin. You can explain it all to your security chief when we're done, and if he has any questions, he can stop by our cabin and ask me about it. How's that?"

Dawson waved them back to the ladderway for cylinder four. The senior porter motioned the others in that direction, and the porters headed for the ladderway down into cylinder four.

Once in their cabin, and the porters gone, Dawson put a finger to her lips, and Morgan nodded. Dawson checked the security feeds via VR, and found the cabins were wired for video and sound. She shut off the video and sound feeds from the cabins of all the passengers aboard and made it look like a system failure on their deck.

They were on deck fourteen of cylinder four, called 4-14 in ship parlance, and their dining room was on this level as well. She shut off the video and sound feeds for the 4-14 dining room as well, and sent a VR message to all the Board members inviting them and their families to a meeting in the 4-14 dining room in thirty minutes.

Finally, Dawson blocked the security codes from operating the cabin doors of all the passengers. The doors would only respond to the cabins' listed occupants. When the Board left their cabins, the cabins would be secure.

"OK, we're good. I had to block all the security surveillance for this deck. Internal Ship Security is out of control, clearly," Dawson said.

"I'm glad you were able to push through it. I wasn't sure you could bluff your way past all that," Morgan said.

"No bluff. They're way outside policy, and they know it and don't care. I'm just as glad we didn't have to fight our way aboard, though."

Dawson started collecting cases of ammo from their dozen or so bags. She had split it up so its combined weight wasn't a telltale to those carrying their luggage. She consolidated all six thousand rounds into one hard-sided case.

The pistols were in another case.

"... or by such other group ..."

Enfield raised his voice to be heard in the crowd of forty-five or so passengers gathered in dining room 4-14.

"Can we have all the Watchers at this one central table here, please," Enfield said. "Everyone else, take a seat at one of these two other tables."

People sorted themselves out and took their seats.

"OK, first things first. How many people here are competent tactical shooters?"

Ten of the Watchers, mostly those in the age range from about thirty to sixty, raised their hands, including Enfield and Dawson herself.

"And how many of you managed to get your personal weapons past security?"

Only four raised their hands, again including Enfield and Dawson.

Dawson put one of the two heavy hard-side cases, 24" x 16" x 8", that she and Morgan had brought to the meeting up on the table and opened it. Morgan brought up the other and opened it. As the hinged lids were flipped over onto the table, the Watchers could see the first held twelve Vandar Elite 8mm platinum-slide semi-auto pistols, thirty-six magazines, a dozen Tacticon Premiere smart holster rigs, and several dozen pairs of Saf-T-Ears electronic ear buds, while the second contained hundreds of boxes of Pegasus 8mm SuperExpander 180-grain platinum hollow-point ammunition.

"First things first then," Dawson said. "Every shooter needs to arm up. Each of these pistols is new, has been meticulously gone over by the best gunsmith on Horizon, and has had two hundred rounds run through it to break it in and ensure operation and accuracy. I'll tell you how thorough he was. He prepped twenty pistols and rejected five."

Eyebrows went up at that. The Vandar Elite had a heavy platinum-alloy slide to soften the sharp recoil from the hot 1500 fps 8mm round and was reputed to be the finest 8mm tactical pistol available, at any price. Five rejects out of twenty pistols would have given Emile Vandar heart failure.

"OK, shooters, come on up and draw supplies. I have five hundred rounds per shooter here, and canvas bags to carry the extra boxes back to your cabin. Let's load up and holster. We need to make sure we're secure first thing. You should probably insert the ear buds now, too. I don't trust Ship Security."

It took fifteen minutes for everyone to draw supplies, load all three magazines, put on the holster rigs, load the pistols, and holster both the pistols and spare magazines. They inserted and activated the ear buds, which were auto-fitting.

When all were reseated, Dawson waved a hand to Enfield, and George Enfield took back the floor.

"All right, everyone. We're monitoring the corridors in VR, and we're armed up. Now that we're secure, let's introduce ourselves. I'm George Enfield, Childers 1."

"Patricia Dawson. Childers 2."

"Bok Jessen. Jessen 1.

"Tracy Carter. Xi 2.

"Janos Anders. Durand 1."

"Bill Chen. Joshi 2."

"Ivan Voorhees. Petros 2."

"Mary Dragic. Bhatia 2."

"Juan Linna. Desai 1."

"Oliver Popov. Petros 1."

"Gretel Gadhavi. Johnson 2."

"Rachel Peters. Murphy 2."

"Sue Niewinski. Turner 2."

"Bob Graham. Murphy 1."

"Monique Minami. Desai 2."

"Jack Turner. Turner 1."

"Sofija Macar. Bhatia 1."

"Natasha Sanna. Xi 1."

"All right," Enfield said. "We all have each other's biographical information from the Galactic Mail central computer systems. Natasha Sanna, at age 91 you are the senior Watcher. You are the interim chair."

"I delegate that task to you, George. You're doing a fine job. Carry on," Sanna said.

"Very well. Thank you, Natasha," Enfield said. "Our first order of business is to elect ourselves as the new Board of Directors. Did everyone receive the VR remote units? Anyone not wearing it now? OK, good. So we can vote with the ship's computer.

"Do I hear a motion?"

"I move we elect this group the Board of Directors of Galactic Mail," Natasha Sanna said.

"Seconded," said Bob Graham.

"I have a motion and it has been seconded. Vote in the VR, Aye or Nay on the motion," Enfield said.

"The motion carries," the computer said from the overhead speakers a few seconds later.

"OK, we are now the Board of Directors," Enfield said. "The next item of business is for the Board to elect its chairman.

"The floor is now open for nominations."

Sanna once again spoke first. "I nominate George Enfield. I asked the computers after the notification came, and he and Patty Dawson here have been the source of a lot of the information we've been receiving the last seven years. Before that, we didn't get much. Also, the remote VR units. And they're the ones who smuggled the guns on board so we could be adequately armed. So I think George is the natural choice."

"Other nominations?" Enfield asked. No one else offered a nomination, because no one really knew any of the other Board members yet.

"Computer," Enfield said.

"Yes, Mr. Enfield," the computer said.

"Can you access the biographies of all the Board members in my private secure storage in the ship's accounts?"

"Yes, Mr. Enfield, with your permission."

"Analyze those biographies for the work experience, education, and age to determine the best candidates for chairman. Figure in the training classes we took as well, and our scores."

"Mr. Enfield, Ms. Dragic, and Mr. Turner have the most relevant experience and education and are in the optimum age range."

"Well, there's our candidates everybody. Now what do we do? Speeches?"

"George, as interim chairman, I call the vote," Sanna said.

"All right, everyone. I'm overruled. Vote in the VR," Enfield said.

"Mr. Enfield has a majority of the vote," the computer said a few seconds later.

"Congratulations, George."

Sanna stood and shook Enfield's hand, and everyone clapped briefly.

"The next order of business is to name a president for Galactic Mail," Enfield said.

"According to the by-laws, you nominate the president, and the Board can concur or demur on your choice," Turner said.

"Computer, based on the analysis of the biographies of the current Board and their scores in training, who are the best choices for president?" Enfield asked the overhead.

"Ms. Dawson is the best candidate, followed closely by Mr. Turner."

"Very well. I nominate Patricia Dawson as president of Galactic Mail. Vote demur or concur in the VR."

"The Board concurs with Mr. Enfield's nomination of Ms. Dawson as president," the computer said a few seconds later.

"Mr. Turner," Dawson said. "Will you serve as vice president?"

"Yes, of course," Turner said.

"As your president, I step down from the Board," Dawson said.

"And, as vice president, I do as well," Turner said.

Enfield took the floor again.

"Per the permanent by-laws, and by our votes, we are the Board of Directors of Galactic Mail, its president, and its vice president. I have requested the central computer system not make this information public, or inform the current leadership. As you know, that was one of our options until we met. I think we should continue that arrangement for the time being. All agreed? Any opposed?"

There were no opposing votes.

"What we need to discuss then is how we proceed from here. It seems to me the first thing we need to do is assert our control over this ship, GMS *Mnemosyne*. With that, I'll turn the floor over to our president."

Under Arrest

As Patricia Dawson walked down the corridor on *Mnemosyne* from the dining room back to their cabin, Marcus Abrams, the head of Ship Security, stepped out of a cross-corridor in front of her.

"Patricia Dawson, you are under arrest."

"On what charge?"

"Conspiracy against Galactic Mail."

"There's no such crime."

"Nevertheless. You will come with me."

Two security guards had come up the corridor behind her. She was logged into the VR through her remote neck pickup and could see the clear corridor beyond them.

"The hell I will. And if you or your two goons make any move against me, I'll kill you all where you stand."

When he nodded to the two guards behind her, for a moment he was looking at them, and they were looking at him. In that moment of inattention, Dawson hit the release on the smart holster through the VR and the pistol dropped from under her blouse into her right hand. With the smoothness of long practice, she double-tapped Abrams in the center of mass as she brought the pistol up and turned, then fired three rounds at each of the two guards in what was still known among tactical shooters as the Mozambique Drill – double-tap to the center of mass and one shot to the head.

She walked over to where Abrams was bleeding out on the floor.

"You should have listened to me."

She put one round into his head, between the eyes.

Dawson scanned the corridor up and down, and checked her near vicinity in the VR. With no one else coming, she dropped the half-expended magazine into her free hand and loaded a full magazine, putting the half-empty magazine in the magazine holster with her second reload. She re-holstered the weapon, and commed the Board through the VR.

"Code Red. Security tried to arrest me. I'm fine. Three down dead in corridor 4-14."

Dawson accessed *Mnemosyne*'s computer in flag-override, locking all the interior doors in brig protocol. They would be unable to be opened from inside or outside without flag authority, which all the Board had.

Dawson and the Board had not yet let on to the captain or crew of *Mnemosyne* that the Galactic Mail central computer systems had given them the flag-override codes for the big ship, or that they had transmitted them and been recognized when coming aboard. Intended for an admiral to take command in dire need, none of the captain or crew had them, and none could countermand them without physically disconnecting all the individual systems on the ship.

Dawson also shut down all access to the interior security monitoring on the ship. Only she and the other Board members would be able to access the camera views of all corridors and spaces.

Finally, she killed all communications through the VR system except for her and the other Board members and their families.

Enfield was walking down a corridor in the command cylinder when he got Dawson's message. He continued walking without showing any sign of being alerted. He was unsurprised when Kurt Schechter, the assistant head of Ship Security, stepped out of a cross-corridor in front of him.

"George Enfield, you are under arrest."

"For what?"

"Conspiracy against Galactic Mail."

"Oh, that." Enfield visibly relaxed, and spoke off-handedly. "You might want to check with your boss. There's been a change of orders."

"I don't think so."

"No, really. It was all a mistake. You should check."

Schechter got a vacant look as he accessed his VR, then became concerned.

"I can't raise Abrams. Hell, I can't raise anybody," Schechter said to the two security guards who had come up behind Enfield.

It was at that moment of distraction, with the three security people all looking at each other and thinking about something else, that Enfield moved. The one in front, two behind scenario was one of the standard practice setups in their tactical shooting exercises. Enfield's actions were a repeat of Dawson's just minutes before, including the coup de grace to Schechter and reloading his weapon.

Enfield commed Dawson and the Board.

"Same here. Three down dead in corridor 1-12."

"This ship is on lock-down. On-watch bridge personnel, maintain your positions. All personnel in quarters and workspaces, remain where you are. All personnel in the corridors, proceed to the nearest crew mess and await further instructions. Anyone remaining in the corridors will be presumed hostile."

The message repeated twice more over the ship's speakers. It was in the captain's voice, but it wasn't his orders. Dawson had constructed the message. And all the interior hatches were secured, so most personnel weren't going anywhere anyway.

Dawson watched crew members heading to the crew messes over her VR link. When they were assembled, she secured the hatches to the crew messes as well.

Dawson had the ship's computer monitor corridors for movement and queue those images for her. More of the Ship Security morons were patrolling corridors and ignoring orders to report to the nearest crew mess. She sent all the info on to the other nine Board members who were proficient tactical shooters, assigning them to specific targets and positions.

George Enfield took up his position just inside a cross corridor, facing away from the mess. Anyone going the wrong way could be presumed hostile. He casually leaned against the bulkhead, and waved and smiled at crew members heading for the mess as they passed him. After most of the crew were assembled in the mess, he continued to VR monitor the corridors in his area for hostiles.

A squad of four Ship Security passed his position at a lope, headed away from the mess toward the ladderways, weapons drawn. He stepped out into the corridor after they passed and double-tapped them all from behind. He walked forward, finished off two who were still breathing, and changed magazines. He picked up an extra pistol and two extra magazines for it from one of the bodies.

"Four down dead in corridor 1-11."

Enfield melted into a side corridor and consolidated his two half-empty magazines into a single full one. That done, he moved to his next position.

Gretel Gadhavi took up a position on 4-15 near the access into cylinder four from the ring corridor above. Any security coming in to cylinder four had to pass through this chokepoint. She watched the ring corridor and the bottom of the ladder in VR.

She watched as a squad of four Ship Security guards came up into the ring corridor from cylinder two, moved around the ring and into the short corridor to the ladderway to cylinder four, and came down the ladder. As the last came down the ladder, with their squad leader talking to them and all of them looking away from her position, she stepped out of the side corridor and began firing.

She double-tapped each of the guards from behind, then took three head shots on those down but still moving. Jack Turner and Lacy Carter moved past her and started up the ladder as she reported in.

"Four down dead on 4-15."

Once in the ring corridor, which the VR showed them was currently clear, Turner and Carter took up positions in the short corridors leading to the ladderways to empty cylinders five and ten. Only cylinder one, the command cylinder, crew cylinders two and three, and passenger cylinder four were currently occupied.

They could see in the VR that Ship Security was getting organized on 2-15, at the bottom of the ladder into cylinder two. There were two squads. They went up the ladder to the ring corridor one squad at a time. When all eight were up the ladder and in the ring corridor, the first squad headed for the cylinder four ladderway.

Turner and Carter coordinated in the VR. At the mark, they both stepped out from their side corridors. Turner's targets were in sight immediately, focused on the short corridor to the cylinder four ladderway, facing ninety degrees from him. He double-tapped them all in the center of mass, then delivered head shots to those down but moving.

Carter was two cylinders away in the vertically curved corridor, and out of sight of the squad at the cylinder two corridor when she stepped out. She advanced down the hallway just as Turner's shots rang out, which kept her targets facing away from her as she came around the ring. She double-tapped them all in the center of mass from behind, then headshot the movers.

The curve in the ring corridor kept Turner and Carter from being in each other's direct line of fire, and the sound absorbing tile on the curved floor squelched any ricochet.

"Eight down dead in the ring corridor."

The VR showed them the remaining squad of Ship Security that weren't locked in. They were trying to hot-wire the hatch to the Ship Security ready room on 2-14. Carter and Turner took the ladderway down into 2-15, then down one more deck to 2-14. Turner went around one way, and Carter the other.

Once in position, just around the corner from the Ship Security ready room, Carter signaled Turner, just around the corner on the other side. Turner fired a single shot. Carter immediately stepped out from concealment to see all four of the last remaining free squad turning away from her down the corridor toward the noise. She double-tapped them all in the center of mass from behind, and finished off two moaners as she walked up.

"Four down dead in 2-14."

Carter and Turner, Enfield and Dawson, Gadhavi and Graham then went from cabin to cabin, workspace to workspace, on deck 2-14, until there was no more Ship Security on *Mnemosyne*.

Captain Bowers

Pat Dawson had Captain Bowers brought to the Admiral's ready room under armed guard. No one on the bridge gave them any trouble, and she re-secured the hatch to the bridge behind them in VR.

George stood careful watch, with Dawson out of his line of fire.

"We have just completed securing your ship, Captain," Dawson said. "Twenty-six of your Ship Security were killed in the fighting. The other thirty-four were trapped in their quarters and ready room when I secured the hatches. We have since shot them and spaced all the bodies. Your crew is all secured in their cabins or the crew messes, which are also locked. Your decision now is to follow my orders or follow Ship Security out the lock."

"How did this melee all get started?"

"Marcus Abrams and two of his goons tried to arrest me. I killed them. Kurt Schechter and two of his goons tried to arrest George Enfield here. He killed them. From there it was 'Game On,' and we killed them. We killed them all. No prisoners, no surrender. I simply don't have time for that, against a superior force, or to try to convince people to see reason only to have them stab me in the back later."

"And we suffered no casualties."

"A dozen or so civilians against sixty armed and trained security personnel? I don't believe you," Bowers said.

"See for yourself."

The display on the ready room wall came to life and showed scene after scene from the security cameras of Ship Security being bushwhacked and gunned down, in threes and fours, by single shooters. These were followed by scenes of the systematic execution – there was no other word for it – of Ship Security personnel who had been locked in their quarters and ready rooms, caught by surprise when the hatches unexpectedly opened and a pair of shooters took them down.

"We've trained for this our entire lives, Captain. For this very eventuality. Trained and expert tactical shooters. Trained in hand-to-hand combat. Trained in strategy, tactics, and ship handling. Trained in your own security procedures. Trained in your own computer systems. Trained with your own training courses.

"Of course, we couldn't have done it without access to your flag-override codes, Captain. So you need to ask yourself: How could I have possibly gotten your flag-override codes? The answer is simple. Galactic Mail's central computer systems gave them to me. Why would they do that? I can answer that question easily.

"Computer," Dawson addressed the overhead.

"Yes, Ms. Dawson."

"Who is the Chief Executive Officer of Galactic Mail?"

"Patricia Dawson is the CEO of Galactic Mail."

"And who is Chairman of the Board of Galactic Mail?"

"George Enfield is the Chairman of the Board of Galactic Mail."

"Has this been confirmed by Galactic Mail's central computer systems on Doma?" Bowers asked.

"Yes, Captain Bowers," the computer voice said.

"You see, Captain. *We* now head Galactic Mail."

"But who are you people? How can you do this? I've never heard of any of you. It's not time for a shareholders meeting or Board elections."

"For that, I'll ask you to look to the display once more."

The display lit up again, with a clip Dawson had made of Jan Childers' VR recording, the one she received when she first signed up as a Watcher.

Bowers watched, fascinated, as an aged Jan Childers explained the role of the Watchers, and why they watched. He watched through to the end.

"... Uniting all of humanity under one government would be a tremendous mistake. Sooner or later, even the most benevolent and well-intentioned government can be corrupted, turn to despotism. To where, then, would one flee to escape it? From what outside point could one oppose it? Humanity would sink into millennia of tyranny.

"We decided the possibility – more, the likelihood – of tyranny on individual planets was a lesser evil than tyranny on the grand scale, across all of humanity. Galactic Mail is structured to prevent a galactic government from forming, as long as it does not become one itself.

"But we believe it will, or at least it will try.

"It is for this reason that you watch. It is your great responsibility."

Bowers turned back to Dawson.

"So you see, Captain. From the very founding of Galactic Mail, there has been a secret group of Watchers, established by Galactic Mail's founders, dedicated to being prepared if and when Galactic Mail strayed from its purpose. To step in and restore it to its original role. To avert the great evil of a galactic central government. For a hundred and seventy-five years, this group has watched Galactic Mail, and trained against the chance they were needed. The eighteen passengers you picked up are the current members of that group. We are the Watchers.

"As for who we are individually, George here and I are distant cousins. We have the same seventh-great-grandmother.

"Our seventh-great-grandmother was Jan Childers, Captain, and we are taking back her legacy. To that end, I will destroy anything I have to destroy, kill anyone I have to kill, to keep Galactic Mail from becoming a galactic tyranny over trillions of human beings.

"You can either help me or I will kill you out of hand."

Bowers looked back at the display, where the image of Jan Childers remained. He had no doubt it was Childers. He had seen her portrait often enough in Galactic Mail facilities. She had aged, but no one could forget those eyes.

Truth be told, he had his share of misgivings about Galactic Mail's new focus. He was old school, and had been with Galactic Mail for thirty years, long before the current regime. Academy training then had included the role of Galactic Mail in the grand scheme of things, and one of the things it was not to be was a galactic government. He had studied enough pre-space Earth history to know where that would end up, and how badly.

He had studied some of Jan Childers' history, too. Always one for long-term plans, it would be just like her to build a safety into Galactic Mail, a mechanism to reset the massive organization to its original purpose. It would also be just like her to use an unconventional and unexpected method to do that.

But could these eighteen people really overturn Galactic Mail, which had almost two hundred million employees? Hell, a third of them were over seventy years old. Then again, they had managed to lock up a crew of thirty-five hundred, kill sixty security guards, and take control of the ship, and on a moment's notice. Of course, override access to the ship's computers made all the difference, but if the computers were willing to give them the overrides to *Mnemosyne*, why would they not give them the codes to all Galactic Mail ships and drones, everywhere?

One other concern was whether or not these eighteen people, pulled from all across human space, were ruthless enough to do what needed to be done, because he knew the leadership of Galactic Mail would be, to preserve their positions. That appeared not to be an issue. One thing Patricia Dawson had shown so far was her capacity to be utterly ruthless, and up close and personal at that. Unusual in a woman perhaps thirty-five years old.

Why should that be? It was the family legacy, he realized. All the eighteen Watchers were the direct descendants of the founders of Galactic Mail. They would not see their families' legacy be perverted, become a tyranny that engulfed all humanity, have their ancestors' names and memories drowned in blood. There would be hell to pay first, and Patricia Dawson seemed more than willing to mount the pale horse and lead hell itself into the battle.

Bowers turned back to Dawson, and the family resemblance to Jan Childers pulled at him. He wondered if this was what it had been like to face the legendary Admiral Childers across a flag ready room table.

"That won't be necessary, Ma'am. I'm on board," Bowers said. "I've had my own concerns about Galactic Mail's recent policies, but as just one cog in the gearing, I didn't see how to make a difference. Now I do. It won't be easy, though."

"I don't expect it to be easy, Captain. I expect it to be hard. But we will prevail. For the sake of humanity itself, we will prevail, at whatever cost."

Now What?

Dawson, Enfield, Turner, and Morgan were in the admiral's flag ready room on *Mnemosyne*. They were monitoring Captain Bower's speech to crew members in the crew mess on deck 2-14. He had already talked to his senior officers and bridge staffers. Dawson had released enough crew from their cabins to fill the 2-14 mess, but the captain would have to give the same speech half a dozen times more to personally address the entire ship's crew.

"Can we trust Bowers? You told him he could either cooperate or you would kill him. Not much of a choice. What do we do if he just made nice, and now intends to lead the crew against us?" Enfield asked.

"I'll use the fire control valves to dump the compartment to space and start over with the first officer," Dawson said. "If I have to, I'll vacuum the whole ship except for our people and call another ship here through Galactic Mail's central computer system. And Bowers knows the fire control system as well as I do."

Fire in a mess hall was a danger to the whole ship. For that reason, mess halls had air-tight doors and fire control valves that could dump the atmosphere in any mess hall to space by means of a central pipe that ran the length of the cylinder through its mechanical spaces. Like sea water on an ocean-going ship, vacuum was inimical to fire, and there was plenty of it available.

"But I don't think that will be necessary," Dawson continued. "Bowers is old enough to remember the Galactic Mail he joined as a teenager. I think he was honest with us about not being on board with the new regime."

"Well, he seems to be doing well enough so far. I don't think we can let the crew have shore leave, though. It only takes one to spill the beans to the current leadership," Turner said.

"Nope. How are they going to let them know? Through Galactic Mail? I'm blocking any news of what we're doing from management," Dawson said.

"I thought Galactic Mail's mail system was inherently secure," Morgan said. "That even Galactic Mail couldn't interfere with delivery of the mail."

"That's true," Dawson said. "But once it gets into the internal mail server at Galactic Mail headquarters, I can get at it. The mail will get there, but it won't display in their inbox when they access it. It's only a holding action, and they can figure it out if I block too many, but there hasn't been anything to block so far."

"All right, so that's sealed off for the time being. The big question is, Now what? How do we proceed from here? Assuming Captain Bowers and his crew is on our side, what we have is this one ship."

"Not quite. I've taken the liberty of beefing up our offensive capabilities," Dawson said. "Computer, what is the current drone complement of *Mnemosyne*?"

"Two hundred hunting parties of ten drones each, two hundred fifty nuclear warhead drones, five hundred kinetic impact drones, and a dozen survey drones."

"Twenty seven hundred drones?" Turner asked.

"I've been skimming the ready drone complement of Galactic Mail deployment centers," Dawson said.

"That's enough to reduce a planet," Enfield said.

"Well, it's enough we don't need to worry about anyone giving us any grief for the time being," Dawson said.

"OK, but the question stands. What now?" Enfield asked.

"Well, I don't think we can just space to Doma and ask the current management for the keys to the building," Turner said.

"Yeah, that probably wouldn't work very well. Why Doma, anyway?" Dawson asked.

"Because that's where Galactic Mail is headquartered," Enfield said.

"Is it?" Dawson asked. "Isn't the headquarters of Galactic Mail wherever the Board says it is? Why go to Doma? That's where the current management is. Why confront the devil in his own lair?"

"Doma will be upset to lose the headquarters. They've supported the current management," Turner said.

"Doma by this point is basically a company planet. It's completely in their pocket. That's a real good reason to occasionally move the headquarters around, by the way," Dawson said.

"So where do we move it to?" Enfield asked.

"I was thinking one of the other bases. Computer, how many bases does Galactic Mail have right now?"

"Including Doma, Galactic Mail has fifty-seven division bases."

"How many of those include research facilities?" Enfield asked.

"Including Doma, twelve of them include research facilities."

"How many of them have shipbuilding and drone manufacturing capabilities?" Turner asked.

"Including Doma, twelve of them have shipbuilding and drone manufacturing capabilities."

"Are those the same twelve?" Enfield asked.

"Yes. All twelve Galactic Mail regional bases have both manufacturing facilities and research facilities."

"Computer, analyze," Dawson said. "Of the bases with manufacturing and research facilities, make recommendations for a new headquarters location for Galactic Mail, considering the quality of the research facility and its staff, the capacity of its manufacturing facilities, and the likelihood of the senior management in place favoring a return to prior Galactic Mail policy with regard to internal system affairs. Equal weighting on parameters. Full analysis."

"Problem formulated. Queued for transmission to Galactic Mail central computers on Doma."

"Computer, expedite. Unscheduled drone authorized," Dawson said.

"Drone dispatched."

Dawson looked around the table.

"OK, so we should hear back within hours. I think we want to go wherever that is, to that regional base, tell the management we're the new leadership team, and then issue press releases announcing Galactic Mail's new leadership and new headquarters location."

"What about Doma?" Enfield asked.

"What about it?" Dawson asked. "Doma continues to be a regional base for Galactic Mail. Operations will be unaffected. We can thank the prior Board and leadership for their service, and just act like everything's all normal and peachy."

"They're not going to let it go at that."

"Of course not. But we won't be the aggressors," Dawson said.

"I like it," Turner said. "Declare ourselves and let them come to us. Make them fight us on our home ground."

"And we'll be ready for them," Dawson said.

"Just to jump in for a second, I like this plan from a legal point of view," Morgan said. "The legal basis for us moving on Doma in force is shaky. The legal basis for the new Board setting up a new headquarters is solid though, as is the legal basis for defending against attack. And any attack from Doma or anywhere else against the new headquarters is an interplanetary incursion, which justifies a response from Galactic Mail. So it's solid all the way around."

"So we're decided that we take this to the Board?" Dawson asked.

She scanned the others and got nods all around.

"I know you're all wondering what's going on, so here it is in a nutshell.

"Galactic Mail has new management. Our founder, Jan Childers, built into the by-laws a mechanism for pulling Galactic Mail back from becoming a galactic government, by replacing the existing management if they went too far astray. That mechanism was triggered by Galactic Mail's recent attack on Wallachia. Whether or not that attack was a good thing is not the point. It was not in Galactic Mail's charter. It was not part of our mission. And it is a step on the road toward tyranny.

"Or so Jan Childers believed. I've just seen a previously unknown VR of her discussing this, and she made her position quite clear.

"So Jan Childers' safety mechanism was triggered, and Galactic Mail has new management. In terms of our responsibilities, to me they are clear. I personally verified the credentials of the new management with Galactic Mail's central computer systems. When I ask Galactic Mail on Doma who the Board is, who the CEO is, then I figure we can take that to the bank. Our oaths are to the organization, not to one group of leadership or another, and when the organization says this is the current leadership, well, there you are.

"As for what happened here on ship, Ship Security, without my authorization, tried to take the new CEO of Galactic Mail into custody. When they ignored her warning, and were about to resort to force to carry out this unlawful act, she killed them. She then locked all of you in your cabins, or ordered you to the crew mess, to remove you from the violence and save your lives. Ship Security persisted in its unlawful efforts to detain the new CEO and Board of Directors. They were unsuccessful, and all of them were killed.

"As for what we do now, it's simple. We do what we have always done. We follow orders from our lawful superiors. We obey lawful commands. We carry out our assigned duties. We uphold the charter and traditions of Galactic Mail.

"And with that, you are all released and ordered back to your normal duty schedules.

"Dismissed."

The next morning, Dawson, Enfield, Turner, Morgan and Bowers met in the flag ready room.

The ship was up and operating normally again, with all ship's crew at their stations. Breakfast in the 4-14 dining hall had been wonderful. There is nothing quite like a meal aboard ship in the first-class dining room.

And the results of the analysis had come back from Doma.

"Computer. You have the results of the analysis I requested last evening?" Dawson asked.

"Yes, Ms. Dawson."

"Report."

"With the parameters you specified, the best candidates for being the new headquarters of Galactic Mail are Pulau, Kalnai, and Odla, in that order of preference."

"How close are those candidates' scores to each other, and to the rest?"

"These three are nearly tied, Ms. Dawson, while the rest follow after a large gap. Together with Doma, they make up the large regional center category, followed by eight small regional centers."

"OK, got it," Dawson said. "Well, everybody, any input on any of these? How do we choose?"

"No clue," Enfield said.

Turner and Morgan shook their heads as well.

"If I might put in a word," Bowers said.

Dawson nodded, and he continued.

"The dozen Titan ships are spread four each among those three large regional centers. *Mnemosyne* and three of her sister ships are based out of Kalnai, and most of the crew is from planets in that region. I know the local regional manager who's in charge on Kalnai, and I think my executive officer served under the operations chief there at one time."

"Where is Kalnai, geospatially?" Enfield asked.

"It's close to the population center of Galactic Mail's service area. It's a really big operation."

"And the regional manager's politics?" Dawson asked.

"I haven't talked to her about it, but I think Kali Micheli has to be outraged. She is more old-school Galactic Mail than I am. I noted they didn't send the attack to Wallachia from Kalnai, but from Doma, even though Kalnai is closer."

"Well, gentlemen. The Board signed off on the plan, and told us to pick which Galactic Mail base to use as the new headquarters. What say you?" Dawson asked.

Enfield looked at Turner and Morgan, and spoke for all three.

"Looks like Kalnai to me," Enfield said.

"All right, Captain. You have your orders. We space for Kalnai when *Mnemosyne* is ready for departure," Dawson said.

"We're restocked, Ma'am, and ready to go. I'll set departure for two hours. Call it 10:00 hours."

A Quick Trip

The passengers were all strapped into the desk chairs in their cabins well before the maneuvering warning sounded in the crew spaces. Stewards saw to it everyone was properly strapped in and everyone had taken their anti-weightlessness-sickness pills.

Dawson was in her cabin with Morgan, but she was logged into the VR and present on the virtual bridge watching the preparations. She was in oversight mode on her flag-override codes, so they could not see her on the bridge, but she could see them.

Of course, *Mnemosyne* had a physical bridge, but it was more for emergency maneuvering if the VR system went down. The bridge-watch crew was also physically present in the physical bridge, strapped into their own chairs. But all the action was in the virtual bridge, within the VR system.

Dawson was watching for any sign of a double-cross. There were things Captain Bowers could do, such as kick *Mnemosyne* to maximum acceleration to try to hold the Board in place while he attempted to retake control of the ship. Dawson had taken a high-g pill just in case. She only needed to hang on long enough to shut down the attempt with her flag-override codes, and *Mnemosyne* was only capable of two g anyway, but prepared was better than not prepared.

But there was no double-cross. The *Mnemosyne*'s bridge was a model of efficiency and professionalism as the ship's rotation was slowed and brought to a halt, the cylinders were folded, and the ship got under way at one-g toward the nearest point of its hyperspace-1 transition envelope.

After three days in orbit, *Mnemosyne* was finally headed out of Horizon space.

Her massive drone complement, kept informed of her movements by survey drones popping in and out of hyper, tagged along in hyperspace-1, unseen.

It was five hours at one g to the hyperspace-1 limit for *Mnemosyne*, so Captain Bowers secured from maneuvering and everyone was free to move around. After a couple of hours, they were served lunch in the 4-14 dining room.

After lunch, Dawson sent a message through the VR to Captain Bowers.

Dawson to Bowers: Captain, when we reach Kalnai, I want to hold in hyperspace while we drop a couple of survey drones into normal space to check that their operational tempo remains unchanged. Sooner or later the previous management of GM will understand something is up and put the word out. I want to make sure that hasn't happened yet before we drop out of hyper. It may change how we proceed. Is that possible?

Bowers to Dawson: Yes. Will comply.

Dawson to Bowers: Excellent. If operational status unchanged in your opinion, make standard approach to the planet. Standard orbit. Routine return to Kalnai. Else hold in hyper and notify me.

Bowers to Dawson: Understood.

Just before 15:00 hours, the porters returned to make sure all the passengers were strapped in for the hyperspace portion of the transit. Dawson once again logged into the bridge via the VR to watch the proceedings.

There was no drama. It was almost mundane. The ship transitioned into hyperspace, the displays reconfigured to show the navigational display and the ship kept accelerating right through the transition.

After thirteen minutes, the ship transitioned into hyperspace-2, then transitioned again at thirteen minute intervals into hyperspace-3, hyperspace-4, hyperspace-5, and hyperspace-6. After only a few minutes in hyperspace-6, at an effective normal-space acceleration of

$(4\pi e)^6$ g, or one and a half *billion* gravities, the engines shut down and Dawson was weightless. She watched the bridge and the exterior views as the *Mnemosyne* flipped ship, and then reengaged the engines for deceleration. A few minutes more in hyperspace-6, and then the sequence played out in reverse, with down-transitions through the hyperspaces at thirteen minute intervals.

After a number of minutes in hyperspace-1, the engines shut off and Dawson was weightless again. Fifteen minutes later, she received a message from Captain Bowers through the VR.

Bowers to Dawson: Kalnai operational status normal. Proceeding to standard arrival orbit.

Mnemosyne's engines reengaged and apparent gravity returned. A few more minutes and *Mnemosyne* transitioned into normal space. The hyperspace warning light went out, and they were once again free to unstrap and move around.

The entire hyperspace portion of the trip, traveling hundreds of light years, took less than three hours.

After dinner in the 4-14 dining room, Dawson met with Bowers in the captain's ready room. Bowers had requested the meeting to brief her on their status and request orders.

"So we will take up our standard orbit around Kalnai, and *Mnemosyne* will report in as having arrived. We will synch our ship's clocks to the time at the Galactic Mail base on the planet, which is about three hours ahead of us currently. The question is, Then what?" Bowers asked.

"Can you get a meeting with Kali Micheli, the regional manager, sometime tomorrow morning?"

"I think so. Especially if I make a priority request for a confidential meeting. Her curiosity will kill her to find out what it's about."

"I think that's what we do then. You schedule a meeting, and then you, I, and George Enfield all go down to meet with her," Dawson said.

"Both you and George? I have to warn you Port Security has had similar issues to what you witnessed with Ship Security here. They are all under the same organization, and the previous Galactic Mail leadership had sixteen years to turn them into something of a regime security force. What if something happens to both you and Mr. Enfield?"

"Then they get to deal with Jack Turner and Mary Dragic, and God help them."

Kalnai

It was 10:00 hours the next morning when they set out for the planetary headquarters of Galactic Mail on Kalnai. Dawson noted with interest the location of the Port Security Building on the base as they came in for a landing on the shuttle pad on the roof of the Administrative Building. The trip down was just over forty-five minutes, and so they were on time for their 11:00 meeting with Kali Micheli.

Dawson had spent an hour this morning familiarizing herself with the layout of the base, its construction, and the ships currently in orbit. One in particular interested her, and she commed that ship's computer with her flag-override credentials and was recognized.

Dawson and Enfield also wore the Saf-T-Ear electronic earbuds this morning. Almost invisible in the ear canal, they contained an active repeater for sound as long as the decibel level didn't exceed safe levels, at which point they interrupted the signal, acting as ear plugs. She offered a set to Bowers as well, and he accepted them with a raised eyebrow.

"Being prepared never hurts," Dawson told him.

They were met at the shuttle pad by an attendant and shown down to the outer office of the regional manager. On the way, Dawson VRed into the base computer systems and verified that the information that the leadership of Galactic Mail had changed had in fact been circulated out from Doma to the regional computers, but was being held confidential by the systems pending her authorization. She also verified that her download from this morning had arrived in her mailbox on base.

At precisely 11:00 hours, the secretary showed them into the regional manager's office.

"Captain Gregory Bowers, Ms. Patricia Dawson, and Mr. George Enfield."

"Come in, come in," Micheli said as she came out from behind her desk. She shook Captain Bowers hand. "It's good to see you again, Greg."

"And you, Kali."

She shook Dawson's and Enfield's hands in turn.

"Ms. Dawson. Mr. Enfield. I don't believe we've ever met."

"No, Ms. Micheli. Not unless you've ever been to Horizon. This is our first time off our home planet."

"Interesting. No, I've never been there. Well, be seated, everyone. Please," Micheli said as she waved a hand to a sitting area off to one side of the office.

Dawson and Enfield judged sight lines to the door and took chairs on the far side of the small coffee table.

When they were all seated, Micheli started off.

"Well, what's this all about then?"

"Before we start, Ms. Micheli," Dawson said, "I should warn you your office is likely under video and audio surveillance by Port Security."

In fact, Dawson knew that to be a fact. While flag overrides did not penetrate Port Security, her CEO authority did. She had been watching Micheli doing paperwork at her desk in real time over the VR while they were waiting in the outer office.

"Oh, I don't think so, Ms. Dawson. Port Security is under my authority, and I have authorized no such intrusion."

"Very well."

On her head be it, Dawson thought.

"We are here," Dawson continued, "to discuss the mechanics of setting up the new headquarters of Galactic Mail here on Kalnai."

Micheli raised an eyebrow.

"Have you been authorized by the CEO or the Board of Galactic Mail to pursue this mission?" Micheli asked.

"Ms. Micheli, I *am* the CEO of Galactic Mail, and Mr. Enfield here is the Chairman of the Board of Directors."

Micheli continued to look at Dawson, but she pitched her face and voice toward the overhead.

"Computer, who are the current CEO and Chairman of the Board of Galactic Mail?" Micheli asked.

"The current CEO of Galactic Mail is Patricia Dawson, while the current Chairman of the Board is George Enfield," the computer voice came back.

"Has that been verified by Galactic Mail central systems on Doma?"

"The information arrived in a secure communication from Doma three days ago, and was released for her use by Ms. Dawson this morning."

"Has this information been made public?

"No, Ms. Micheli."

Micheli lowered her head back down to face directly at Dawson and simply stared.

"George Enfield and I are distant cousins, Ms. Micheli. Our seventh-great-grandmother was Jan Childers," Dawson said, nodding toward the picture of Childers on the wall to her left. "The founders of Galactic Mail built into its by-laws and its structure a mechanism for their descendants to take control of the corporation if it strayed too far from its charter. They expected Galactic Mail to eventually try to devolve into a galactic central government, and they set up a protection mechanism against that eventuality. Galactic Mail's attack on Wallachia, placing Galactic Mail's authority over a planetary government's in its own internal affairs, was deemed sufficient departure from its charter, sufficient motion toward a galactic government, to trigger this mechanism.

"Consequently, the eighteen descendants charged with keeping watch on Galactic Mail have taken control of the corporation."

"That is an incredible story," Micheli said.

"It's just the sort of thing Admiral Childers would do, though, Kali," Bowers said. "I know you've studied her history, too. We've talked about it. And I saw a pretty incredible clip of her discussing this whole thing. The whys, hows, and wherefores."

"I've sent you a short VR file of Jan Childers discussing the matter, Ms. Micheli. We would be pleased to wait while you viewed it," Dawson said.

"Please. I would find that most helpful," Micheli said.

"Go ahead, Ms. Micheli. You, too, Captain Bowers, if you wish. You've seen a 2-D clip, but I sent you the VR file as well."

Micheli and Bowers got distant looks on their faces as they accessed the VR with their own VR remotes. Jan Childers looked at her watch. Shouldn't be too long now.

At the end of the clip, Micheli's and Bowers' focus returned to the here and now. Micheli broke the silence.

"That was an incredible experience, Ms. Dawson. To see and hear Jan Childers discuss her plans, extending centuries into the future. What incredible clarity of vision. Thank you for that."

The door from the outer office burst open and five men in the uniform of Port Security swarmed into the room. Micheli and her guests stood up.

"Mr. Sitko, what is the meaning of this?"

Kian Sitko. He's the head of Port Security. Good, Dawson thought.

"Sorry, Ma'am. Patricia Dawson, George Enfield, you are under arrest."

"On what charge?" Enfield asked.

Enfield and Dawson walked forward, to place themselves slightly in front of Micheli and Bowers, who had been seated between them and the door. They needed to clear their sight lines.

"Conspiracy against Galactic Mail."

"There's no such law," Enfield said.

"Nevertheless, you will come with me."

"Go fuck yourself," Dawson said.

Sitko flushed with anger, but he merely nodded to his team, and all four guards started forward.

The obscenity was a signal from Dawson to Enfield. They drew as one, and Mozambique drilled the four security guards, each taking their own side of the foursome. The guards were still falling when two shots hit Sitko in the head almost simultaneously. His gun had barely cleared the holster, and clattered as he fell.

"My God," Micheli said.

Dawson walked to the door, and closed and locked it. She turned back to face Micheli.

"Well, I did warn you," Dawson said.

Dawson used the VR to trigger the command file she had downloaded this morning, and several things happened at once. All the Port Security personnel got a VR message from Sitko's account, in Sitko's voice, calling them to the Port Security Building for an emergency meeting. The VR system then shut down messaging to or from all Port Security personnel so they could not communicate.

And in orbit, a single kinetic weapon drone detached from the GMS *Magellan*, which was just now approaching the Galactic Mail Kalnai regional base in its orbit. The *Magellan* was on planetary rotation, being restocked and with much of its crew on planet leave. The standby bridge crew watched helplessly, unable to stop the weapon from launching seemingly on its own.

"What do we do now?" Bowers asked.

"We wait. I've set some things in motion, and there's nothing to do until they play out," Dawson answered.

When no backup squad showed up, Dawson and Enfield holstered their weapons. Micheli was still staring at the bodies on the floor.

"I can't believe you could just do that. It was all so fast."

"We've been training for this our entire adult lives, Ms. Micheli," Dawson said. "Against the chance that, during our time on watch, Galactic Mail would go off the rails. And it clearly has. You thought Port Security was under your authority, but in fact they serve only the regime of Sylvain Costa."

Micheli tore her gaze away from the bodies to look at Dawson.

"Actually, I think this is more the work of Padma Kosar, Costa's chief of staff. Sylvain isn't as big of a problem as she is. He's the political face, the smooth operator, but she's the iron behind it. The corruption of the security organization is likely her work."

Dawson checked the VR, and looked out over the base toward the Port Security Building.

"I think what we should do at the moment is to get behind Ms. Micheli's desk here. In case the windows don't hold," Dawson said.

Micheli looked confused at that, but Bowers had caught the direction of Dawson's look, and he motioned Micheli toward the desk.

"Down on the floor here, Kali. I think there's more fireworks on the way."

All four of them got down on the floor on the side of the desk away from the big picture window. Dawson kept an eye on events in the VR.

"All right. One minute. Cover your head with your arms, just in case," Dawson said.

Dawson had allowed fifteen minutes for all the security personnel to make it to the Port Security Building, where they all waited for Sitko to come and tell them what was going on.

The kinetic weapon drone had initially accelerated toward the planet for two minutes at its full ten-g acceleration, then shut down and came in ballistic. Just short of the Port Security Building, it exploded. Rather than a single large hit in the center of the building, there were dozens of hits spread across the building. The building imploded, collapsing in on itself, and the burning fragments of the drone set the debris on fire.

The Administrative Building shook to the impact, and then the blast wave hit the building. The windows held. Dawson had checked the base construction, and she knew all the windows on the side of every building facing the shuttle field were reinforced against a shuttle explosion. Port Security had built its headquarters in isolation across the field from the rest of the base, so the impact on the Port Security Building was in exactly the direction the reinforced windows of all the other buildings protected against.

Dawson had also used the option to explode the drone prior to impact, to maximize the effect on the building while minimizing the shock wave. The multiple smaller hits at different distances from the other buildings spread out the shock in time, but reduced its peak amplitude.

Dawson and the rest stood up from behind the desk and looked out the picture window to where the rubble of the Port Security Building blazed on the other side of the field.

"How many Port Security people do you think were in the building?" Bowers asked.

"Almost all of them. I sent out a message to all Port Security personnel over VR, from Sitko's account, in Sitko's voice, recalling everyone to the Port Security Building, no sooner than the gunfight here was over," Dawson said.

"But how did you know?" Micheli asked.

"I didn't. But it was one of the possibilities, so I set up some options in my plans."

"Port Security was almost six thousand people."

"Ms. Micheli, Galactic Mail stands poised to become a galactic government that will doom trillions of people to tyranny for millennia. I will not allow that to happen. I will destroy whatever I need to destroy, I will kill whoever I need to kill, to keep that from happening. To keep Jan Childers' legacy of peace from being perverted into a hundred generations of oppression."

Dawson pointed out the picture window.

"Consider that destruction out there, from a merely ballistic drone, and then consider the destruction Galactic Mail caused on Wallachia, with three full-power kinetic strikes in the middle of a major city and two ten-megaton warheads dropped on major police bases. And that's just a taste of what's coming if we don't stop it.

"So I ask you, Ms. Micheli, are you with me? Do you stand against tyranny, or do you stand aside?"

Micheli looked out at the ruins of the Port Security Building, drew a deep breath, and seemed to stiffen. She drew herself up straight and turned back to Dawson.

"No, I'm with you, Ms. Dawson. You've had years to consider the issue. For me this has all unfolded in a single hour. But I'm with you, you and Jan Childers. I didn't like where things were going. I didn't like the Wallachia strike. I didn't like the Port Security situation, though I had no clue it had gotten so far out of hand. But I didn't see what I could do about it. And now I do.

"So what's next? I know you have a plan, just as Jan Childers would have."

"Actually, I have her plans, drawn up by her staff almost two hundred years ago. And, believe it or not, there's nothing that's happened so far they didn't see coming.

As for what's next, I need your help with that."

Ship Security

Jack Turner and the remaining fifteen members of the Board sat in the flag ready room aboard *Mnemosyne*, waiting for word of what was happening on the planet. Dawson, Enfield, and Bowers had been gone less than two hours when they heard from Dawson over the ship's comm, relayed through the VR system to their remote pickups.

Turner and the Board members had been working on the Ship Security problem all morning.

There were hundreds of Galactic Mail ships in orbit around Kalnai. Freighters of all sizes in the process of unloading or loading, drone tenders on ready status for deployment in case of an attack on a shareholder planet, the three big Titan liners that were sister ships to *Mnemosyne*, the smaller liners that spaced under the Galactic Mail banner. Every one of these Galactic Mail ships had a Ship Security contingent.

For each ship design, they formulated a strategy. For most it was a message calling an emergency meeting of Ship Security in the mess hall on the deck Ship Security occupied. Ship Security were to arm up and report to the mess hall. They were to tell the mess hall staff to leave because of the confidential nature of the meeting.

Of course, which deck Ship Security occupied on each ship was different among ship types. Separate messages had to be composed for each of them.

Some ships had small security contingents, and it was enough to call them all to the ready room, which was actually the surveillance room aboard ship. On some others, messages were composed requesting all Ship Security to report to their quarters and arm up, then await instructions.

When the comm came in from Dawson, they were ready.

When Dawson commed just before noon to say they had neutralized Port Security and the Ship Security portion was a go, Turner triggered the transmission of downloads to the ship's computers of all Galactic Mail ships in Kalnai space. He followed this up with multiple communications transmissions to each ship, relayed through the Galactic Mail headquarters.

"Ma'am, incoming orders from Kalnai dispatcher."

"Go ahead," said Captain Katalin Kang, captain of the GMS *Tethis*, one of *Mnemosyne*'s sister ships.

"It's a general order, Ma'am. No Galactic Mail ships are to depart the Kalnai system for the next twelve hours."

"Well, we weren't going anywhere anyway. Curious order, though. I guess they'll let us know what is going on whenever they're ready. Maintain station."

"Yes, Ma'am."

Lintao Mendes, head of Ship Security on *Tethis*, was hurrying his subordinates to the mess hall.

"But he can't mean to leave the ready room unoccupied," Paul Radic said.

"I'm not going to tell Kian Sitko what he means and what he doesn't mean. Come on, let's go. We're just going to be down the hall, and we can monitor everything in VR anyway. Move it," Mendes said.

"Yes, Sir."

Kian Sitko, as head of Port Security in Kalnai, was Mendes' ultimate superior in the region. Ship Security constituted deployed units of Port Security, and the promotion path to a cushy planet-side job ran through Kian Sitko's office.

They all filed into the mess hall, to "await an important live message from Kian Sitko." Mendes ordered the mess hall crew out for the confidential meeting, as ordered, and all sixty Ship Security personnel on *Tethis* were present and accounted for at 12:15.

At 12:16, the bulkhead hatches to every Ship Security cabin and workspace on Tethis locked in brig protocol.

At 12:17, the bulkhead hatches to mess hall 2-14 on Tethis closed and locked. Fifteen seconds later, the fire valves for mess hall 2-14 dumped the air to space.

All across Kalnai system space, the scenario repeated itself. Ship Security personnel were locked in their ready rooms and quarters, or they were executed in their mess halls. Over two thousand died, and another thousand were locked up.

The big ship had shuddered when the fire valves had opened in the mess hall on 2-14, but Captain Kang was still trying to figure out what was going on when the lieutenant on communications interrupted.

"Ma'am, we have an emergency communication from Kalnai. It's Kali Micheli on a broadcast communication to all ship captains in Kalnai."

"Put it on the display, Mr. Knutsen."

Micheli's image appeared on the display. She waited a few seconds more before beginning.

"To all Galactic Mail captains in Kalnai space.

"Galactic Mail has new leadership. The new Board of Directors is all composed of descendants of Galactic Mail's original founders. The new Chairman of the Board is George Enfield, the seventh great-grandson of Jan Childers. The new president and CEO of Galactic Mail is Patricia Dawson, the seventh great-granddaughter of Jan Childers.

"I have checked their credentials, and personally verified their claim directly with Galactic Mail's central computer systems on Doma. This new leadership was triggered under Galactic Mail's by-laws in response to the unlawful and unauthorized attack on Wallachia. Our founders have reasserted control of Galactic Mail through their descendants.

"As we were about to announce this new leadership, Port Security here on Kalnai moved to arrest CEO Dawson and Chairman Enfield. Port Security was secretly monitoring my office. Ship Security was secretly monitoring your cabins, ready rooms, and communications as well. They reported directly to Security headquarters on Doma, around Galactic Mail's official leadership, directly to the prior CEO and his chief of staff. Call me naive, but this came as a shock to me.

"In response to Security's attempt to revolt against the lawful leadership of Galactic Mail, we have taken action to neutralize this insidious force within our company. The Port Security Building on Kalnai has been destroyed. Most Port Security personnel perished in that explosion, and the rest are being rounded up.

"On your ships, most Ship Security personnel have been locked in their quarters and ready rooms, or perished in their mess halls as we lured them in and then blew out the air with the fire control valves. These were lawful actions against them for their treason against Galactic Mail's charter and its leadership.

"On your ships, you should round up any of Ship Security who remain. They must either surrender or be destroyed. We are reasserting our leadership over Galactic Mail, and removing this dangerous personal police force of the former leadership.

"When all this is sorted out, I look forward to welcoming each of you to Kalnai to meet Galactic Mail's new leadership. Until then, let us rededicate ourselves to Galactic Mail's goals, and thank heaven for the wisdom of its founders, who saw this crisis centuries in advance and built in the mechanism to see us through it.

"Micheli out."

"Wow."

"You can say that again, Mr. Knutsen," Captain Kang said.

Kang motioned her executive officer over.

"Tim, let's go ahead and re-pressurize the mess hall on 2-14 now we know it wasn't a fire. Get a body count. Let's see how many Ship Security people we have left to round up."

"Yes, Ma'am."

The attack on Ship Security wasn't perfect, though. Some Ship Security personnel slipped the net. On thirteen ships, they took over the ship by occupying the bridge and holding the captain and bridge crew hostage to their commands. Those ships attempted to leave Kalnai space at their orders.

In each case, a Board member took direct control of the ship through flag overrides, locked out the bridge controls, and directed the ship's computers to space to a holding area well clear of the planet. A hunting party of *Mnemosyne*'s drones then dropped out of hyper around each ship.

Kali Micheli demanded the surrender of Ship Security on each of these ships. The holdouts on ten of the ships complied. The other three ships, all freighters, were blown out of space.

Research

Micheli arranged for Dawson and Enfield to have a briefing from Research that afternoon as she was dealing with the clean-up of the situation with the (former) Security personnel on Kalnai and the Galactic Mail ships in-system. She also had to take a somewhat frantic call from the chief executive officer of the Kalnai government, who was called simply the Chair.

"Perhaps you could tell me first what you are most interested in hearing about, Ms. Dawson," said Austin Misra, the head of Research for Galactic Mail on Kalnai.

"Two things mostly, Dr. Misra," Dawson said. "First, what is Galactic Mail on Doma likely to have that we do not have here, and second, what do we have here that is unavailable to Galactic Mail on Doma."

"You expect to have a confrontation with Doma?"

"It's on my list of short-term expectations, yes."

Misra nodded slowly at that. Micheli had included Dawson's and Enfield's current positions and how they had come by them in her introductions before she had scurried off.

"Let me tell you first, Ms. Dawson, that students of science are often students of history as well. We have become more and more concerned with the situation in Galactic Mail over the last twenty or so years, and I think I speak for most of us in Research when I say we're delighted you're here."

Misra looked over the other three people he had brought with him to the briefing, and they all nodded.

"With that as a background, let me start with a comparison of our efforts to that of Research on Doma. We believe we are significantly ahead of them in our efforts here, and have been for a very long time. Partially that is because Galactic Mail's central organization has become complacent. The primary goal of a stable and successful organization over the long-term is to maintain the status quo, so aggressively researching additional capabilities, which, after all, might be destabilizing, is not a priority.

"One might expect there to be more than a little bias in my opinion on such matters, but in this case, I think it's correct. Unless they are hiding things from us, which is a possibility, they have little on the table in terms of undeployed new technology. I weigh the possibility they are hiding things from us against what I see of their attitude when we get together for conferences. They seem, well, less than motivated.

"Indeed, most new deployed technology within Galactic Mail for the last fifty years or so has come from this facility, as well as our friends on Odla. We have a little bit of a technology competition going on with them.

"As for what we have in the shops, we are always working on longer-range beam weapons, smaller and cleaner nuclear devices, higher-speed drones, that sort of thing.

"But I suspect what you will be most interested in is our work on a higher-speed drone tender."

"What is its acceleration?" Dawson asked.

"Five gravities is pretty routine."

"Really."

"Yes," Misra said. "The standard drone tender acceleration has been just under three gravities for generations. There just was not a good way to make a human-occupied ship faster and still have the humans aboard remain, um, operational. We think we've solved that problem."

"And that is how, exactly?"

"For the standard drone tender, the human crew already occupies flotation beds and runs the entire ship in VR. We've taken that passive mitigation system a step further by constructing an active system. The entire crew is maintained in water-filled tanks, and breathe through a scuba-type apparatus. We use a piston system to pressurize the tank to an effective depth of forty meters. Are you with me so far?"

"Yes. So sixty-five psi or so. Say 4.5 bar," Dawson said.

"Excellent, Ms. Dawson. Exactly so. Now, the crew is in the tanks, and breathing through that scuba-type system, which we call COSS, for Crew Oxygenation and Scavenging System, and they are controlling the ship through the VR."

"And five gravities?"

"As the engines are engaged, the pressure at the bottom of the tank increases due to the high apparent gravity. As it advances the engines, the ship's computer manipulates the piston system to maintain the pressure in the tank at a constant," Misra said.

"So the body feels no effects of the acceleration at all."

"Not quite, Ms. Dawson. For thirty minutes under a pressure that is the equivalent of a forty-meter dive, the body requires ninety minutes to decompress back to normal pressures. Now, the crew is still in control of the ship during that period, but the acceleration of the ship during that period will be limited to the current pressure in the tank plus a discomfort factor."

"Or, you could sit doggo for a couple hours in hyper and de-pressurize," Dawson said.

"Correct. But you also have to allow enough time between pressurizations, and you can't keep pressurizing and de-pressurizing. You need to allow time for the residual nitrogen to be processed out of the body, otherwise it becomes very dangerous. One gets a sort of nitrogen poisoning, which scuba divers call the bends."

"But it does give the capability for five-gravity maneuvers when required."

"Within the time constraints of what the body can stand as far as pressure, yes," Misra said. "We're still working on the exact curves. We're currently testing operating at lower pressures, at around three bar, but there is some discomfort associated with higher accelerations. Alternatively, we could keep the pressure at 4.5 bar and operate the ship as high as seven gravities. The engines themselves are good for eight gravities at one hundred percent. We've actually done a couple of runs at seven gravities, and that's worked out so far. We're still doing test runs and analyzing data, but that's a possibility for you.

"And the atmosphere mix people are breathing makes a difference, too. We think we can get away from using nitrogen altogether, which might solve some of the depressurization problems."

"And of course you have accelerations of less than three g available pretty much all the time."

"You mentioned thirty minutes under pressure, Dr. Misra. How far can a five-gravity ship travel in thirty minutes in hyperspace?"

"The ships are hyperspace-7 capable, Ms. Dawson. At five gravities, you can go anywhere in the galaxy in thirty minutes."

"Wait a minute," Dawson said. "You said 'the ships *are*?'"

"Yes. We have four of them."

"You have a whole *division* of these?"

"Yes, of course," Misra said. "Did I not mention that? After all, we have to be experimenting with something to get any reliable results."

"And they're operational now? And have crews?"

"Yes. That's right. Ready when you are, as they say."

Dawson flopped back in her chair and thought furiously about how to use the new capabilities. Primarily as surprise, she expected. And you only had thirty minutes. Still....

"Does Doma know you have this capability?" Dawson asked.

"Well, I think we may have forgotten to mention it to them somehow."

Dawson raised an eyebrow.

"As I say, Ms. Dawson, many of us are students of history as well. It just seemed, ah, prudent to have some capabilities Doma did not know about."

"Indeed. Anything else I should know about?"

"One more thing you might find interesting, Ms. Dawson. We have the ability to find and track ships in hyperspace, but it has very short range."

"How short a range?" Dawson asked.

"Not more than four light-months or so."

"Four light-*months*?"

"Yes," Misra said. "You can't use it to, say, find someone a light-year away. But gravitational signatures are magnified in hyperspace. A ship in hyperspace-6, we can see four light-months away, in hyperspace-5, four light-days away, in hyperspace-4, three light-hours away, in hyperspace-3, six light-minutes away, in hyperspace-2, twelve light-seconds away, and in hyperspace-1, only about point-four light-seconds away."

"OK, so the range to a ship you can see goes as the hyperspace constant."

"Yes. Correct again." Misra looked to his colleagues, who were all smiles, and back. "I must say, it's much more pleasant to brief someone who is so well studied, Ms. Dawson, as opposed to the more bureaucratic types."

Dawson waved a hand in a gesture of dismissal.

"I read a lot," Dawson said.

"Indeed. And now my colleagues can give you a detailed briefing on each of these areas of our capabilities, in which they are the project leaders."

Preparation

The Board and their spouses and dependents moved down to the planet that first afternoon, and were staying in VIP accommodations contained within a wing of the main administrative building. Captain Bowers returned to the *Mnemosyne*.

The next morning, Dawson, Enfield, Turner, Micheli, Micheli's second, Rada Sato, her head of Tactical, Otto Sokolov, and her chief of staff, Dev MacConnel were meeting in Micheli's conference room. Several other Board members who had trained up on strategy and tactics were also present, including Bob Graham, Mary Dragic, Gretel Gadhavi, and Natasha Sanna.

"Why don't we start with a summary of Galactic Mail's field organization, Kali? We need to know a bit more about the lay of the land," Dawson said.

"Certainly, Pat," Micheli said. "The way the regions are organized, each of the eight small regional centers are loosely administered by one of the four large regional centers, like Kalnai. The other forty-five headquarters, the divisions, report to one of the regional centers. So I have loose authority over Bugaro and Cartref, but really each regional commander is his own boss reporting to Doma. The three of us each have three or four divisions reporting to us, as well as running division-level operations out of our own regional base.

"So the map of Galactic Mail is actually fifty-seven separate territories, over five of which I have administrative control and over another nine of which I have some oversight. The other three large regional centers, including Doma, are set up the same way.

"As for the other three regional centers, I know the managers of each of those. We coordinate a lot. On Doma, there is a regional manager below Galactic Mail's central administration, who has the same authority as I and runs her own region as independently as any of us do. I know her as well as the others.

"It's not necessarily the way anyone would set it up from scratch, but Galactic Mail sometimes grew really quickly, in lurches, and during that process, that's how it ended up."

"Ok, let me see if I've got this," Dawson said. "You have your five divisions, including one based here, plus you have two small regional headquarters and their total of nine divisions, including two that are co-located with them, under your more-or-less control. And you know the other three large regional managers personally, and each of them has the same span of control as you."

"That's right."

"So you could order your five divisions to do something, recommend it to your small region managers for their nine divisions, and suggest it to your peers at the other large regional headquarters."

"That's basically it. I normally wouldn't take direct action in any of the other fifty-two divisions on my own initiative," Micheli said. "You could, though. Everybody reports to you, through one channel or another."

"What does everybody think? Jack?" Dawson asked.

"So there's two paths, right? You can send drones and messages and command routines to all fifty-seven divisions directly, neutralizing the Port Security and Ship Security forces the way we did here, or you could work through channels. If you work through channels, we could miss divisions, maybe a large number of divisions, in clearing out Security."

"And if you act directly in all fifty-seven divisions without working through local managers, you could turn a large number of them against you," Enfield said. "That wouldn't be good either."

"No, it wouldn't. There may be a better first step, though. We need to prepare to be attacked here by Security forces loyal to Padma Kosar," Dawson said.

"Can't we just take over their ships through flag overrides?" Turner asked.

"My suspicion is Kosar has ship-based forces that do not contain flag overrides and respond to her personal command alone," Dawson said.

"Why do you think that?' Turner asked.

"Because it's what I would do in her place. Because there are huge funds missing on Galactic Mail's books. Because Jan Childers and her staff noted it as a possibility. All of the above," Dawson said.

"I didn't notice the missing funds," Enfield said.

"Don't forget I'm an accountant."

Micheli's eyebrows went up at that.

"Actually, I think Pat's right," Micheli said. "It would be just the sort of thing Padma Kosar would do. When she realizes something is going on out here, she's likely to send battle squadrons our way."

"Kosar already knows something is going on out here," Dawson said.

"How?" Enfield asked.

"Because Sitko and every other Security commander reports to Doma every day, and he didn't send a report yesterday afternoon."

"Should we send fake reports? Keep them in the dark?" Enfield asked.

"I don't think so," Dawson said. "First thing is, it's the weekend, and no reports are expected Saturday and Sunday anyway. Second is, sooner or later, we're going to have a showdown with Kosar's forces. Having that showdown before we take out Security in the other divisions is probably better, because our attacks on Security then will not be unprovoked. I want to keep the record clear."

"But there's no strategy for fighting ships of equal capability as Galactic Mail's. There's never been anyone of equal capability to fight," Micheli said.

"There's never been anyone of equal capability to fight, but that doesn't mean there isn't a strategy," Dawson said.

"Well, I've never seen one," Micheli said.

"Jan Childers, Tien Jessen, Jeannette Xi, Bev Bhatia, and their staff developed a strategy, and ran it on simulators. They kept it secret, but it's in our instructions, the plans they set aside for the Watchers. I've already set it in motion.

"The first step is to gather our forces.

"Then we're going to poke the bear."

The meeting became a tactical planning session that ran over three days, with Otto Sokolov's tactical people in and out of the room constantly, running simulations of different scenarios.

Dawson and Morgan were having dinner the night of their second day on Kalnai.

"I've been thinking. I think we need to bring the kids here, Hon," Dawson said.

"Into the center of the maelstrom?" Morgan asked.

"They'll be safer here than on Horizon. I worry about Padma Kosar trying to get at me through the kids. Kidnapping them. Or worse."

"You think she would do that?"

"Based on what I've heard, I don't think there's much she'd stop at to preserve her power in Galactic Mail. I want them here where I can protect them," Dawson said.

"What about your mom?"

"Up to her. If she wants to come along, that's OK. I'll mention it to her in my mail. She probably won't, though. You might suggest she visit friends or something for a week or so if she doesn't come along."

"OK, Patty. I can run out to Horizon and get them. Only take a couple days," Morgan said.

"No. There are a couple of small VIP courier ships here. You can run out there and back in less than a day. I'll let Mom know you're coming. I'll send a special dispatch mail drone."

"You're in a hurry."

"Things are going to be moving very quickly," Dawson said. "I don't know how long we have before Kosar goes off. And I want you back here before it all hits the fan."

"All right. I can leave tomorrow morning early, and be back for a late supper."

"I appreciate it, Hon."

The VIP courier ship was a three-gravity vessel, though they made the trip at a more leisurely 2.5 gravities. Bob Morgan spent the five-hour trip in a flotation tank, and was on the ground in New Hope by 9:00 hours local time.

He messaged Pat's mother, Claire Vogel, from the airport that he was on his way. When he got to Campbell Hall, Claire, the kids, and three suitcases waited on the porch.

"Daddy! We're going to go on a spaceship?"

"Yes, Billy, we're going to go on a spaceship."

"Wow!" both kids said in unison.

"So you're coming along, Claire?" Morgan asked.

"Oh, I might as well, Bob. Patty's gonna need a babysitter anyway, and I'm sort of curious about the trip. I've never been off-planet. So it's something new to try."

"You ready to go then?"

"Yep. The house is all closed up and we're all set."

They all bundled into the hired car and headed for the airport.

They were in the shuttle at the New Hope spaceport before 10:00 local time, and landed on the shuttle pad of the administrative building at Galactic Mail's Kalnai regional headquarters by 19:00 hours local time there.

"Mom!"

"We were on a spaceship."

"And we were weightless."

"And they put a tube in my privates so I could pee."

"And their VR let us watch the bridge and everything."

"And they gave us a pill to take with dinner."

"And they said we're gonna have to poop afterwards."

"And grandma came, too."

"Yes, yes, dears, I know, I know," Dawson said as she hugged her chattering kids. The twins tag-team-rattled when they were excited.

Dawson turned to Vogel.

"Thanks for coming, Mom."

"No problem, dear. Just one less thing for you to worry about, and I can help out with the kids."

"OK, well, it's dinner time, so let's go get something to eat."

With her family around her, Dawson felt grounded and at peace. She slept very well that third night on Kalnai.

By the end of their fourth day on Kalnai, Dawson was ready.

Gathering Forces

The tactical resources of Galactic Mail in the Kalnai region – all fourteen divisions reporting directly or indirectly to Kali Micheli – were under the direct command of Otto Sokolov on Kalnai. Dawson wouldn't be stepping on any toes in pulling together Galactic Mail's military resources from across the region.

Across all fourteen divisions, all Galactic Mail drone tenders on ready status received orders for them and their drone complements to space for Kalnai.

The crews of drone tenders on planet re-stock and rotation were recalled as their ships were called to assume ready status. Once their crews were all aboard, those drone tenders, too, spaced for Kalnai.

Ready-status drones in all fourteen headquarters systems dropped into hyperspace and headed for Kalnai.

And in all fourteen systems, freighters containing Sokolov's considerable reserves began offloading drones, thousands of drones, which dropped into hyperspace and headed for Kalnai.

"All right, Jack. You ready to go?" Dawson asked.

"All set," Turner said.

"Be careful. Don't take any chances. Do the job and then get the hell out of there."

"Understood. Hey, I'll be back in a few hours. Don't worry."

"I've got kids. I always worry."

Jack Turner was taking the GMS *Quicksilver* to Doma. *Quicksilver* was one of the new high-speed ships fitted with the acceleration tanks. They wouldn't be pressurized on the way to Doma, to preserve their pressurization allowance, but they would be running like hell coming back.

The shuttle took him up to the ship. It looked to his eyes like any other drone tender. Crew of about a hundred, and, rather than the folding cylinders, it had a single crew cylinder at the rear, around the main engine. There was a hyperspace projector at the front, looking like a smaller version of the main engine, surrounded by the familiar rings of supply and reaction mass containers. It did look like the main engine was longer than the one on a normal drone tender, but he had only had fleeting glimpses of one of those.

The Quicksilver spun around an axis perpendicular to its length, providing apparent gravity in the crew cylinder aft. The shuttle docked in its latches amidships, on a bulkhead that was counter-rotated to be stationary with respect to the shuttle. The crew assisted him in getting aboard ship from the shuttle in the zero-g, and onto the elevator down into the crew spaces.

"Mr. Turner. Welcome aboard. I'm Captain Jola Park," Park said.

"Pleased to meet you, Captain."

"I understand we're in something of a hurry, so let's get you right to your cabin. The nurse will assist you."

"Thank you, Captain."

Park waved Turner toward a fellow in a medical uniform, who led him down a hallway on the bridge deck.

"Right in here, Mr. Turner. And then if you would please disrobe."

Turner stripped down to his skin and the nurse rubbed him down with an oily lotion.

"This coating will keep your skin from getting all wrinkled and waterlogged during the trip. We have a special soap that releases it for your shower when you get back."

At a motion from the nurse, Turner got into the tank. It was about thirty inches tall, and he would be lying on the bottom of the tank a few inches off the floor. While he was still standing, the nurse gave him a high-grav pill and assisted with the single plumbing connection. The nurse then fitted him with a breathing mask.

"It's my understanding you have experience scuba diving, Mr. Turner?"

"Yes. That's why I was chosen. I'm the only one of us, apparently."

"Good. That makes things a little easier. All right, let me put this on you now. Can you breathe OK?"

Turner nodded. The mask wasn't a normal scuba setup. It was a full-face sealed clear mask with two air tubes that circulated air. The air was at a bit of pressure, to hold the seal on the mask, which was also aided by a line of a thicker version of the body lotion. There was also a sippy tube in the corner of his mouth.

"All right. I need you to lay down on the bottom of the tank, and I'll want you to check your VR connection. You can just signal me with a thumbs up once you're sure you're connected.

"Make sure you stay hydrated during your time in the tank. You should drink about six ounces of water per hour.

"If you have any problems during the flight, there is an emergency call button within the VR interface. And we will also be monitoring your vital signs, as well as those of everyone else aboard. Ready to try it?"

Turner nodded and submerged himself in the tank, laying down on the bottom. It was somewhat form-fitting, with a cradle for his head. He belted himself in on the bottom and lay out full-length. He tested the VR, and logged in without trouble. He also tested his breathing with several normal breaths.

Turner gave a thumbs up to the nurse. The nurse's voice came back through the VR.

"Very well, Mr. Turner. I'm going to seal you in now. My own tank is next door, and you have the emergency call button if you need it. Have a good crossing."

With that, the nurse closed the pressure-tight hatch that was the top of the tank. Turner felt a little stir in the water as the air at the top of the tank was pumped out and replaced with water. In his normal senses, he was locked in water in near-darkness, there being a night light in the tank, while in the VR, he had the run of the ship, all its sensors and computer files, and its exterior cameras.

Turner would not leave the tank until he was back at Kalnai.

The tank pressured up a bit, like being in perhaps ten feet of water. Turner watched the virtual bridge in the VR as the *Quicksilver* halted its rotation, engaged its engines, and headed for the hyperspace-1 limit for a manned ship. She was making 2.5 gravities. When Turner dialed back the VR, he felt the additional gravity somewhat, but nothing like 2.5 gravities. He dialed the VR up again, into full immersion, and checked his command files and the plan he was to follow.

After two hours accelerating to the hyperspace-1 limit, Quicksilver transitioned into hyperspace. The transitions occurred at five-minute intervals, all the way to hyperspace-6. They were in hyperspace-6 for several minutes before flipping ship and reversing the process.

After an hour in hyperspace, Quicksilver dropped out of hyperspace in the Doma system twenty light-seconds out, and on the other side of the planet from its ready drones standby point.

As soon as Quicksilver dropped out of hyperspace, Turner presented his credentials to the Galactic Mail central computer systems. They recognized him, and he was in. He downloaded his command files to his secure account, then started the master command file running. He waited until he got an acknowledgement, then watched as the first of the command files executed.

"All right, Captain Park. I'm done. Let's go home."

Quicksilver dropped back into hyperspace and the tank pressured up over the next few minutes. As it did, the engines increased their acceleration until they were at seven gravities.

The hyperspace trip back to Kalnai took twenty-five minutes, while the trip from the hyperspace-1 limit to planet orbit was cut to seventy minutes, as Quicksilver kept cutting its deceleration as Turner and the rest of the crew gradually depressurized.

The entire flight back took just over an hour and a half.

The nurse unlatched the tank and opened the top hatch. He helped Turner out of his breathing gear and his plumbing connection, then gave him a hand getting out of the tank. With the body oil still on his body, he felt like he had been immersed in lard for five hours. The nurse directed him to the shower and he washed off the oil and felt more like himself. He got dressed, and the nurse showed him back to the captain's ready room.

"How was your flight, Mr. Turner?" Park asked.

"It went very well. What an interesting experience. I find it hard to believe we actually went to Doma and returned in five hours."

"Oh, we were there, all right, Mr. Turner. I was starting to get pretty nervous by the time you said to go. It's the most heavily defended planet in the galaxy, and drones were maneuvering to sight on us once we ignored their challenges."

"Really."

"Oh, yes. We had about twenty more minutes before we would have had to bug out in any case. But you got your job done quickly, actually several minutes faster than what I was briefed to expect, and I was happy to be gone."

Turner reported in to Dawson in the conference room that had become their tactical headquarters.

"How'd it go? Any problems?" Dawson asked.

"None at all. Captain Park said their drones were trying to range on us, but I was done with twenty minutes to spare," Turner said.

"And the computers accepted your credentials?"

"Yep. No issues I could see. All the command files uploaded OK, including the master command file, and I checked them all, then kicked off the master."

"Excellent," Dawson said, then checked her watch. She had one time display set to Kalnai and one to Doma, which was a trick because their days weren't the same length, but the watch had all thirty-five thousand human planets programmed into it.

"So now we see what happens," Dawson said. "You ready to get your group together and get off-planet?"

"All set. I already sent them notice of my arrival in VR. They're getting their things together. And Natasha Sanna and Bob Graham are getting their group together."

"Good. I better go say goodbye to my husband and kids."

Jack Turner, Mary Dragic, and half the Board of Directors were taking a shuttle up to the GMS *Magellan*, while Natasha Sanna and Bob Graham were taking the other half of the Board up to the GMS *Hudson*. They had to protect against the possibility the attack from Doma would break through their defenses. It only took one drone with a ten megaton warhead to take out the base. With two ships in space, each with a backup president, a backup chairman, and half the Board, the Watchers as a force would survive such a catastrophe. Leaving all their eggs in one basket on Kalnai was not an option.

Bob Morgan, Billy, and Penny would be going aboard the *Hudson* until the battle was over.

Poking the Bear

The tactical resources of Galactic Mail in the Doma region – which constituted fifteen divisions reporting directly or indirectly to regional manager Kajus Phan – were under the direct command of chief of Tactical Gani Broz on Doma. Orders in her name went out from Doma to all divisions in the Doma region except the division headquartered on Doma itself. She didn't send those orders, the computers did, running one of Turner's command files. That command file was the first one triggered off by Turner's master command file when it's time of execution was hit, before Turner and *Quicksilver* even returned to Kalnai.

Across all fourteen divisions, all Galactic Mail drone tenders on ready status received orders for them and their drone complements to space for Kalnai and place themselves under the command of Otto Sokolov on Kalnai.

The crews of drone tenders on planet re-stock and rotation were recalled as their ships were called to assume ready status. Once their crews were all aboard, those drone tenders, too, spaced for Kalnai.

Ready-status drones in all fourteen headquarters systems dropped into hyperspace and headed for Kalnai.

And in all fourteen systems, freighters containing Broz's considerable reserves began offloading drones, thousands of drones, which dropped into hyperspace and headed for Kalnai.

Padma Kosar was having her weekly meeting with Myron Kwan, the head of Galactic Mail Security. It was their normal Tuesday afternoon meeting, held in her office in the Galactic Mail central administrative building on Doma.

"So what have you got for me this week, Myron?" Kosar asked.

"Not much. We didn't get a report from Kian Sitko Friday, and again yesterday," Kwan said.

"On Kalnai? Again?"

"Yes. I should probably relieve him, but, other than his occasional lapses with reports, he's very good at his job. I'd hate to lose him. I was going to wait one more day, see if he reports this afternoon, before I called him on the carpet about it."

"Well, he's your report, so it's your call. Just don't go too lax on him. Reporting is important," Kosar said.

"Understood."

"Anything else?"

"One curious thing," Kwan said. "Last night we had a ship drop out of hyperspace about twenty light-seconds out, just sit there for about twenty minutes, and then drop back into hyperspace."

"They didn't answer challenges?"

"No ID beacon signal, no answer to challenges. We moved to range the vessel, but they were in a bit of a dead zone in our patrols. Before we could range it, they dropped back out."

"Curious. How big was it?" Kosar asked.

"As far as we can tell, it was a small vessel, about the size of a drone tender or a large yacht."

"Well, probably nothing. But keep a sharp eye on things. Maybe rearrange our patrols a little bit, upgrade our operational status, to get some extra ships or drones out there and close up some of those dead zones."

"Yes, Ma'am," Kwan said.

"Anything else this week?"

"No, Ma'am. That's it."

The second command file triggered off by Turner's master command file installed regular reporting of the system status of the Doma system to Dawson on Kalnai. The complete system map, location and status of all ships, and all ships and drones inbound and outbound in the Doma system were regularly monitored already, the command file simply started a regular reporting of that information. It was updated every half-hour by the regular courier drones that maintained communications among Galactic Mail's fifty-seven headquarters locations.

"So what are we seeing so far, Otto?" Dawson asked Sokolov as she walked into the tactical headquarters Wednesday morning.

She checked her watch. Galactic Mail headquarters on Doma was about four hours behind at the moment.

"They've increased the number of drones maintaining station around the system, and put a couple more drone tenders on ready status on patrol. That's it so far," Sokolov said.

"OK, so they've responded to our little incursion overnight Monday."

"Looks like."

"What about our resources?" Dawson asked.

"Everything has come in, Pat. As each group has come in, we've assigned them a patrol location in hyperspace. I've put them on stand-down status for now, even while they cruise their patrol positions."

"Has our story been holding about an upcoming war games exercise?"

"Yes, we've gotten some pushback. Captains maintaining its silly, Galactic Mail has no large adversaries to war game for," Sokolov said.

"They've grown soft. Well, that will change. And the drones?"

"All holding in hyperspace, Ma'am. It's starting to get crowded out there."

Dawson chuckled. She checked her watch again.

"Good. Very good. Well, it shouldn't be long now until the bear wakes up."

Sylvain Costa couldn't get into the Galactic Mail VR system this morning. His login was refused. He had accessed his account on the display in his office, and had received a single mailed letter instead of a login. He was simply staring at the display when Padma Kosar exploded into his office.

"What the hell is this shit?" Padma said, throwing a printout on Costa's desk.

Costa read the first paragraph while Kosar stood fuming, laid it back on his desk.

"I wish I knew," Costa said.

"It's signed by some Patricia Dawson. Never heard of her. She claims to be the CEO of Galactic Mail."

Costa motioned toward his display.

"I just received a letter informing me I have been removed as CEO by action of the Board of Directors. It's digitally signed by George Enfield, whoever that is, claiming to be the Chairman of the Board."

"Computer," Kosar shouted at the overhead. "Who is the CEO of Galactic Mail?"

"Patricia Dawson is the Chief Executive Officer of Galactic Mail," the computer voice answered from the speakers.

"Well, we can still ask the computer questions, at least," Costa said.

"Who is the Chairman of the Board?" Kosar asked.

"George Enfield is Chairman of The Board of Directors of Galactic Mail."

"Where are they?" Kosar asked.

"Ms. Dawson and Mr. Enfield are at Galactic Mail headquarters on Kalnai."

"Kalnai?" Kosar said.

"Computer, provide short bio on Patricia Dawson and George Enfield, with specific regard to Galactic Mail."

"Patricia Dawson and George Enfield are the seventh great-grandchildren of Jan Childers. Patricia Dawson is an accountant and George Enfield and his brother own an agricultural services company. They are two members of the Watchers, a group put in place by action of the Board of Directors, per Galactic Mail's by-laws, to ensure Galactic Mail does not overstep its charter. The Watchers elected themselves the Board of Directors of Galactic Mail, removing the prior Board, and installed George Enfield as Chairman. George Enfield named Patricia Dawson as Chief Executive Officer and the Board concurred."

"When and where did these Board actions occur?" Costa asked.

"Aboard GMS *Mnemosyne*, in orbit around the planet Horizon, on Tuesday of last week."

"Horizon is where Childers retired. Enfield and Dawson are Childers' seventh great-grandchildren?" Costa said to Kosar.

"I don't give a damn if that bitch is Julius Caesar's twelfth cousin twice removed on his father's side," Kosar said.

"Padma, it's over."

"Bullshit it's over."

"The computers control everything. We have no way to fight this".

"The computers don't control everything. I have my own resources."

And with that, Kosar stormed out of Costa's office.

A Private Navy

Without access to Galactic Mail systems, Kosar couldn't contact Myron Kwan directly. She had to ask her assistant to contact him and ask him to come to her office. By the time he made it over from the Security Building, she was in a cold fury.

"What's going on?" Kwan asked.

Kosar just handed him the letter. Kwan read it, handed it back.

"Who is Patricia Dawson?" Kwan asked.

"An accountant from Horizon. That's where Childers retired generations ago. Apparently she's a descendant. And she thinks she can waltz in here and take over because she doesn't like where Galactic Mail is going."

Kosar put a little emphasis on the word accountant. There was always a danger in a power struggle that some key person would jump the wrong way, go over to the other side. But Kwan's position with Galactic Mail had been very lucrative for him, in ways that couldn't stand a lot of scrutiny, particularly from an accountant.

"That's pretty ambitious."

"Well, it's not happening. I want to take that bitch and her cronies out, and I don't care if we have to burn Kalnai to the ground to do it," Kosar said.

"Kalnai?"

"That's where they're at. That's probably why we haven't had any reports from Sitko. He's gone over to them. I told you he was unreliable."

Kwan shrugged.

"Perhaps."

"In any case, we need to take them out, even if we have to destroy Galactic Mail's Kalnai regional headquarters to do it."

"Well, we certainly have the firepower to do that."

"We probably can't use any regular forces for it, though. They have control of the damn computers. So it's time to call in our little private navy."

"Orders?"

"Go to Kalnai in overwhelming force, demand their surrender, and, when they refuse, take them out. I want that bitch dead."

"What if they surrender?"

"Then I'll be disappointed."

"They've sent out a bunch of unscheduled drones. Looks like thirty of them," Turner said, looking at the display.

"Calling in their forces. Good. Very good. We'll probably have to go to ready status pretty soon," Dawson said.

Drone tenders orbiting Doma recalled their crews and began spacing for the hyperspace limit, to join their ready-status comrades. Also at the hyperspace limit, freighters were unloading thousands of drones.

Warships with their drone complements began dropping out of hyperspace in the Doma system. They did not approach the planet, but stayed at the hyperspace limit. Big cruiser destroyers, much bigger than the drone tenders, with their own firepower, as well as six hunting parties of drones per ship.

"What's it look like so far?" Dawson asked.

"Looks like fifty or so drone tenders, and maybe sixty ships the computer calls cruiser destroyers. Total drone deployment looks like almost ten thousand," Turner said.

"How is that drone deployment split?"

"Looks like thirty-six hundred for the Security ships' drone complement, and six thousand or so for the regular forces."

"All right, let's go ahead and put everybody on active status. They could drop into hyperspace at any time."

"Yes, Ma'am."

Kosar watched her assistant's office display with glee as the big Security ships started dropping out of hyperspace. And, to her surprise, the regular forces ships were responding to Myron Kwan's override orders to deploy for the mission. Over a hundred ships, and ten thousand drones prepared for deployment. And Myron Kwan was in personal command of the mission, so there would be no screw-ups.

That'll fix that bitch, Kosar thought.

The Battle of Kalnai

Orders went out to the assembled ships. Another of Jack Turner's command files had been running in the internal mail system, and it saw the message it had been waiting for. It split the addressees into two different groups, and substituted a very different message in the mail going to the regular forces.

The regular forces of Padma Kosar's deployment would space to Odla, and place themselves under the orders of the Odla region manager and her chief of Tactical.

"All right, let's not go in fast and stupid. Drop a sensor drone into normal space and let's take a look-see what's going on," Myron Kwan said.

"Yes, Sir."

His force was sitting dead-stop in hyperspace-1 at the Kalnai hyperspace limit for manned ships.

"Ma'am, a sensor drone just dropped out of hyperspace," one of Otto Sokolov's sensor techs said.

"OK, he's here," Dawson said. "Everybody act normal. Nobody here but us chickens."

"Ma'am?"

"Old joke. Maintain status."

"Yes, Ma'am."

Dawson waited in what she called her "Enshin mode." Beginning of the bout, waiting for the order to start, centered, ready to react.

"Ma'am, that drone just hypered out."

"Stay sharp, everybody."

"Sir, the sensor drone's back. Kalnai is at normal operational levels. I don't see any evidence of any changes. Drone tenders on station look like they are on a three-in-four peacetime rotation."

"All right. Let's drop out of hyperspace and head toward the planet."

Orders went out to the fleet, and the sixty Security cruiser destroyers dropped out of hyperspace into normal space.

"Sir, the drone tenders? They're not here, Sir."

"What do you mean, not here."

"Just what I said, Sir. We dropped out of hyperspace, and all sixty cruiser destroyers show ready, but the drone tenders aren't here."

Figures, Kwan thought. Their orders must have been messed with by the central computers. But the Security ships' orders were backed up by a separate communication that didn't go through the central computers. Kosar had planned well. He still had sixty ships, and thirty-six hundred drones, in his attack force.

"Doesn't matter. We have more than enough firepower to do this job. Make for the planet, one gravity. Transmit surrender demand as planned."

"They're accelerating toward Kalnai, Ma'am. One gravity," the sensor tech said.

"What I don't understand is, Why bring ships at all? They're sitting ducks. Don't they get that?" Sokolov asked.

"Don't forget. To secure the planet, they need manpower. There's probably eighteen or twenty thousand security personnel on those ships," Dawson said.

"But shouldn't they wipe out any defenses first? Before they cross the hyperspace limit?"

"That's why we showed them a normal operational posture. They don't think there are any defenses to worry about."

"Surrender demand received, Ma'am. They demand our surrender, or they will bombard the headquarters," the sensor tech said.

"Ah, good. We have them on record. Send our surrender demand, Comm."

"We've received a surrender demand from Kalnai, Sir. Surrender or be destroyed. It's from Patricia Dawson, Sir."

"An accountant demands our surrender? What's she going to do, audit me? Repeat our surrender demand."

"Response received. They've spurned our surrender demand and repeated their surrender demand, Ma'am."

"Execute Attack Plan A."

Galactic Mail maintained a total drone complement sufficient to deploy a single hunting party of ten drones per human planet. This was decided early on as a good number, and they stuck with it. With a current total of thirty-five thousand human planets, that meant three hundred and fifty thousand drones, spread out over Galactic Mail's fifty-seven division headquarters, or about six thousand drones per division.

Patricia Dawson had gathered up the drone complement of twenty-eight Galactic Mail divisions to Kalnai, for a total of over one hundred and sixty thousand drones.

One hundred and twenty hunting parties of ten drones each were assigned to Kwan's ships, two complete hunting parties per ship. Twelve hundred drones dropped out of hyperspace five light-seconds removed from the Security formation and opened fire. All sixty ships were hit a dozen or more times and they all disintegrated.

Fifty thousand drones dropped out of hyperspace at their hyperspace-1 limit around the planet and accelerated toward a high orbit around the planet, to form a last-ditch defense against incoming drones. They were programmed to fire on anything that moved between their high planetary orbit and the drone's hyperspace-1 limit.

The other one hundred thousand-plus drones swarmed hyperspace between the drone's hyperspace-1 limit and the debris of Kwan's erstwhile attack fleet, seeking out the attack force's drones in hyperspace. The sensor drones had been reprogrammed to process their sensor data according to Dr. Misra's algorithm for detecting ships in hyperspace by looking for their gravitational signatures. Against such a small target as a drone in hyperspace-1, the detection distances were absurdly short, as little as a few hundredths of a light-second. But the massive wall of drones spaced out across the incoming attack vector swept across the attacking drone squadrons like a net, destroying as they went.

While the drones were small targets, accuracy was good because the distances were so short. It was made simpler because the attacking drones were not programmed to fire in hyperspace, and so the wall of defensive drones received no answering fire.

As each attacking drone was destroyed, and its hyperspace generator destroyed, it fell out of hyperspace into normal space.

"Keep a count on that drone debris. we need to know we got them all," Dawson said.

"We're trying, Ma'am. The computers are having trouble sorting all the data, it's all happening so fast, and they're so close to each other, but we'll get more detailed data back from the sensor drone in each hunting party once they drop out of hyper."

Ten drones made it through the sieve somehow and began attack runs on Kalnai. Hundreds of drones in the last-ditch defensive shell fired at each, and no debris survived to hit the planet.

"Couple of squeakers, there," Enfield said.

"Yeah, but they didn't get through. Let's turn the drones around and get them to sweep back in this direction," Dawson said.

"All right. We think we're close on the count. We're still collecting data from the sensor drones," Sokolov said.

"Well, let's just sweep back anyway. I don't want any stragglers out there."

"Yes, Ma'am," Sokolov said.

"Do you think she threw everything she had at us?" Enfield asked.

"I think so. I hope so. I tried to piss her off enough to get her to commit everything. I would hate for her to have a significant force left and be smarter about how to use it."

The sensor drones began their sweep back. They were about a third of the way back when Sokolov spoke up.

"We've confirmed the count, Ma'am. We got them all."

"OK, good. Let's let them finish their sweep anyway. What's going on around Doma? Anything new?"

"Nothing new there, Ma'am."

Dawson spoke to Enfield.

"Maybe it's time you and I go pay a little visit to Mr. Costa and Ms. Kosar," Dawson said.

Confrontation

The GMS *Quicksilver* dropped out of hyperspace at the hyperspace-1 limit for manned vessels in the Doma system. It was Thursday morning on Doma.

A scan of the system showed the freight operations continued unabated, but there was no military presence in the system at all. No cruiser destroyers, no drone tenders, no weapons drones. Courier drones were arriving and departing continuously, binding together all the planets humans had settled in a single mail network.

Quicksilver headed toward orbit around the planet.

Dawson logged into the central computer system on Doma, and used her CEO authority to punch through the security barriers around the video and audio surveillance archives. She watched the confrontation between Sylvain Costa and Padma Kosar in his office, and the meeting between the late Myron Kwan and Kosar the day before.

Amazing that Kosar would allow her own office to be surveilled. Dawson thought of two alternatives. One was that Kosar didn't know, and it was Kwan's insurance policy. The other was that Kosar thought it would be useful, something she could use, particularly if someone thought she wouldn't be recording her own office.

Dawson also saw Sylvain Costa's departure from the Administrative Building the day before, when he had said goodbye to his staff and wished them well.

On a hunch, Dawson looked for surveillance feeds from the CEO's residence, and found them. Sylvain Costa was at home at the moment, in his home office, and appeared to be emptying his desk.

As *Quicksilver* settled into its orbit around Doma, Dawson commed Padma Kosar on the display in Kosar's office, the first time it had worked since early yesterday morning. She was speaking in the VR, and the computer sent the VR image and voice on.

"Kosar."

"Good morning, Ms. Kosar. Patricia Dawson here."

"You! What are you doing here? Left when it got hot in Kalnai, did you?"

"No, the battle is long over, Ms. Kosar. I came to express my regrets your friend Myron Kwan is deceased. Along with the fifty thousand or so of your Security people he brought along to Kalnai."

"Bullshit. There's no way you could have defeated that force. I sent over a hundred ships and ten thousand drones to Kalnai."

"Then where are they, Ms. Kosar? I'm here, and they're not. Expected to hear something by now, didn't you? You don't look like you slept well.

"As it turns out, all the regular forces you sent to Kalnai got my orders, not yours. They spaced to Odla, and placed themselves under the authority of the regional manager there. And I pulled all the drones and ships in Kalnai region and Doma region, except for those here in Doma itself, to Kalnai well before I sent your termination notice. When your forces dropped out of hyperspace into Kalnai, there were over a hundred and sixty thousand drones waiting.

"It didn't go well for them."

Kosar's display switched to the battle recording by one of the sensor drones as twelve hundred drones fired on Kwan's sixty ships and they disappeared.

Kosar got redder and angrier as this little speech went on. Dawson found it fascinating to watch. Kosar kept enough of a grip, though, to go on through clenched teeth.

"So what do you want from me?"

"Your surrender, Ms. Kosar."

There were transmission delays due to the distance. Dawson knew when her message had gotten to Kosar, though, because Kosar completely lost it.

"Fuck you, bitch. I'll tell you what you'll get if you don't get your ass out of Doma. I have a ten-megaton warhead hidden on this base, and I'll set it off if you don't get your ass out of here. There are three million people in this valley, as well as all the central computers, and I'll blow them all to hell unless you get back on your high horse and get the fuck out of here."

Dawson sent instructions to Turner while she continued to talk to Kosar.

"But that would kill you as well, Ms. Kosar."

"You're going to kill me anyway. If you don't get out of here, I'll take them all with me. Then it'll be on your head, bitch. Three million dead. All on you. So fuck you."

Galactic Mail was currently on the other side of Doma from the *Quicksilver*'s position in orbit, and communications were being relayed by satellites around the planet. The transmission delays gave Turner time. He reported to Dawson on another channel.

"There are only two construction projects that occurred since Kosar came to power that could hold such a device. One in the basement of the Administrative Building, and one in the basement of the Security Building. For everything else, the volume is accounted for."

Turner flipped a map of Galactic Mail's Doma base onto Dawson's screen. The Galactic Mail central Administrative Building and the Security Building were both newer buildings on the far side of the field from the main operational headquarters of the Doma division, at the east end of the huge complex.

Dawson gave instructions to Turner while continuing her conversation with Kosar.

"Are there any conditions under which you would consider surrender without setting off your device, Ms. Kosar?"

Sensing weakness, Kosar pushed harder.

"None whatsoever. As a matter of fact, I have two such devices. If I set them both off, they'll probably kill millions of people in Nadezhda, too. And they're buried, not an air burst. With the prevailing east wind here, the fallout alone will be terrible."

"I'm sorry to hear that, Ms. Kosar."

"No doubt you are bitch. Now get the fuck out of here."

"There's just one thing you haven't considered."

"What's that? Women and children and all that shit? Fuck them."

"No. It's that I don't really care all that much about the computers."

The two kinetic weapon drones came down at a thirty degree angle out of the west, passing fifteen miles above Nadezhda, thirty miles away. They were running at their full ten-gravity acceleration, much faster than the noise or shock wave of their passage. One hit the front of the Administrative Building, the other the front of the Security

Building, at their full power. Both huge buildings collapsed with the initial impact and the explosion that followed with the release of all that kinetic energy.

The angle of incidence made the explosion and all the ejected debris plume out to the east, away from the rest of the people and buildings on the huge base, and the sheer size of the field protected them further. There were damage and injuries on the rest of the base, both from the explosions and the shock wave of the drones' passing over the base, but they were surprisingly light compared to the total destruction of the Administrative and Security Buildings.

Sylvain Costa was in his home office in the front of the house on The Hill west of Galactic Mail's Doma headquarters. The Hill was one of the foothills of the large ridge that separated Galactic Mail's Doma facilities from Doma's capital city of Nadezhda to the west. There was a gap in that ridge, through which the highway and light rail connection between Galactic Mail and Nadezhda ran, and The Hill was just north of the gap, with a splendid view of the base.

When the base was initially built, three large houses had been built on The Hill, looking east out over the base. The three houses were built for the CEO of Galactic Mail, its head of Defense Operations, and its head of Mail and Freight Operations.

Costa was going through his desk, sorting through mementoes of his time at Galactic Mail. He had no doubt that time was over. The computers controlled Galactic Mail. It was impossible to be otherwise. Sure, Galactic Mail employed two hundred million people, but with a customer base of six trillion people spread across thirty-five thousand planets, two hundred million was a small number. High levels of automation were required. If Patricia Dawson and her group of Watchers controlled the computers, they controlled Galactic Mail.

Costa thought of Padma Kosar and shook his head. He had always liked the aggressive chief of staff. She got things done. And if she bent the rules a little doing it, well, so what? He had learned not to inquire too deeply into her methods, satisfied with the results.

But she had clearly gone around the corner. There was no way to resist someone who had control of the computers if they were half competent, and, despite Kosar's sneering dismissal of 'the accountant,' he suspected Patricia Dawson was more than a little competent. The way she had manipulated Kosar's notorious temper was proof enough of that.

His meandering thoughts were interrupted when the whole house shook, hard. Small items fell over on the bookcases and the windows rattled. He looked out the big window overlooking the base, and saw two streaks that passed over the house descending on the base. He just had time to drop to the floor and cover his head with his arms when the ground shock wave and then the air blast wave of the explosions shook the house twice again, even harder.

Costa climbed shakily to his feet and looked out over the base. The Administrative Building and the Security Building on the far side of the base, almost on the horizon, had been converted to piles of burning rubble as a double mushroom cloud lifted over Galactic Mail.

I guess the new administration is here, he thought. *Padma pushed too hard, once too often.*

Sylvain Costa

Dawson stepped out of the shower aboard *Quicksilver*, and donned her best business suit. She sat in the captain's ready room and placed a call to Sylvain Costa in the CEO's residence on the Hill. She had to unblock his display to do it.

Costa was sitting in his desk chair, looking out at Galactic Mail's Doma base, thinking of the loss of his staff and everyone else in the Administrative Building. He jerked, startled, when the display on his desk abruptly came to life with an inbound call.

"Sylvain Costa."

"Hello, Mr. Costa. I'm Patricia Dawson."

Costa responded with what was on the top of his head.

"Was that really necessary, Ms. Dawson?"

"I'm afraid it was, Mr. Costa. Padma Kosar claimed to have two ten-megaton nuclear warheads secreted on the base, which she threatened to detonate."

Kosar's image came on the screen.

"Fuck you, bitch. I'll tell you what you'll get if you don't get your ass out of Doma. I have a ten-megaton warhead hidden on this base, and I'll set it off if you don't get your ass out of here. There are three million people in this valley, as well as all the central computers, and I'll blow them all to hell unless you get back on your high horse and get the fuck out of here."

And then a second clip.

"As a matter of fact, I have two such devices. If I set them both off, they'll probably kill millions of people in Nadezhda, too. And they're buried, not an air burst. With the prevailing east wind here, the fallout alone will be terrible."

Costa had no doubt it was Kosar. He recognized her choice of vocabulary.

Dawson came back on the screen.

"We actually located the devices from construction records, Mr. Costa. One is in the basement of the Administrative Building, and one is in the basement of the Security Building. I have directed warhead disposal units to the scene, with maps to locate the devices."

Costa looked down at his desk and shook his head. What had Kosar been thinking? She was mad. He looked up at Dawson.

"I had no knowledge whatsoever of those devices, Ms. Dawson. I appreciated Padma Kosar's ability to get things done, and was not as mindful of her methods as I should have been. This, this was madness."

"Actually, Mr. Costa, I believe you. I've done my own share of checking into both of your histories. I believe Padma Kosar kept her own counsel, pursued her own ends, without your knowledge. As for your friends and others within the administration who were killed, Kosar gave me only bad choices. I could kill a hundred thousand people, have her kill millions, or leave this base and its resources in the hands of a madwoman. I chose."

"So what do we do now, Ms. Dawson?"

"What I would like to do is to arrange a peaceful – to the extent it can be, now – transition. You know, outgoing CEO welcomes new CEO, handshakes, pictures, press release. The whole thing. It makes things simpler going forward."

"And what then becomes of me, Ms. Dawson?"

"Honored former CEO, living out his life in retirement, the whole happily-ever-after thing. Oh, there might be some quiet auditing done, perhaps a return of some funds, depending on what the audit finds, but not prosecution, not penury, not infamy."

"A generous offer."

"Mr. Costa, I have something of a vested interest in not beginning a new tradition with regard to the treatment of former Galactic Mail CEOs. It could prove, well, inconvenient in the future."

Costa chuckled, the first time he had laughed since yesterday.

"Yes, I see, Ms. Dawson. Well, I'm very good at handshakes, and I'm told I photograph well."

Over the next several days, Costa proved as good as his word. He was everywhere. Overseeing the work of search and rescue crews. Consoling the loved ones of those who had died. Being in every way the concerned and engaged CEO, caring for his company and his people.

Whenever Dawson's actions came up, he defended her vigorously.

"My, God, she saved us all. When Padma Kosar went mad, she threatened to blow up the entire base – three million people – with a nuclear warhead arranged to be dirty. The blast and fallout would have killed many of the thirty million people in Nadezhda as well. Thank God Patricia Dawson was in a position to stop Padma Kosar. We would all be dead. All our friends. All our loved ones. Our children."

When the warheads were actually found, in the places Turner had predicted, Costa judged it the proper time to release the entire conversation between Patricia Dawson, calm and level-headed throughout, and the raging Kosar.

In particular, Kosar's final terrible words – "What's that? Women and children and all that shit? Fuck them." – cemented the truth in everyone's mind.

For the grieving families, Costa accepted liability on behalf of Galactic Mail, for both the failure to see Padma Kosar's developing insanity and the terrible toll it took. To cover its liability, Costa directed Galactic Mail to make generous wrongful death payments, which he sweetened with a substantial donation of his personal funds.

Costa also took personal responsibility for his failure to foresee or avert the tragedy, and announced he would step down as Galactic Mail CEO, as soon as he had taken what steps he could to mitigate it. All attempts to talk him out of stepping down failed.

Dawson suspected the substantial donation would prove to be only part of what would end up being clawed back by the audit, but it was masterfully done nonetheless.

And she signed off on all his actions behind the scenes, to make them all valid under the by-laws.

It was a masterwork of public relations. By the time the transition ceremony was held, both Sylvain Costa and Patricia Dawson were heroes to the employees of Galactic Mail on Doma and their families. No other choice for the incoming CEO would have been so well received.

The ceremony itself was small, a large celebration so soon after the deaths of so many being inappropriate. It would normally have been held on the ground of the Administrative Building. That being impossible, it was held in the gardens of the CEO's residence on the Hill, and broadcast to all Galactic Mail employees on Doma. The recording was also mailed to all Galactic Mail employees throughout all fifty-seven divisions of the company.

With Galactic Mail's origins within the Commonwealth Space Force of the Commonwealth of Free Planets, both long since defunct, the incoming CEO swore an oath to defend the charter of Galactic Mail. Again, in the somber mood after the disaster of Padma Kosar, there were no speeches.

In five minutes it was done, and Patricia Dawson was the publicly acknowledged CEO of Galactic Mail.

It was less than a month since the *Mnemosyne* had picked them up on Horizon.

Sylvain Costa and Patricia Dawson sat in the small seating group in Costa's home office in the CEO's residence on the Hill. Dawson's swearing-in was the first time the two of them had actually met, and this was their first private conversation. Things had been moving too fast, they had both been too busy, in the two weeks since Kosar's fiery death.

Dawson had been back to Kalnai in between, checking in on the transfer of Galactic Mail corporate files from the undamaged data center on Doma to Kalnai, kicking off a forensic accounting team looking into Galactic Mail's books and Kosar's mails, and approving a set of initial parameters for the design of a new corporate Administrative Building on Kalnai.

Dawson had met Costa's wife, Vivian Johnson, and one adult daughter who still lived at home, as well as the Doma region manager and the Doma division manager. She was on-planet with her own nascent staff, borrowed from Micheli's regional headquarters on Kalnai, as well as Enfield and Turner. They had been shown every consideration by Costa, his family, and the household staff.

At the moment everyone else was out in the garden, enjoying the nice day, in a little reception after the transfer ceremony.

"So here we are, Mr. Costa. I wanted to express my personal appreciation for your efforts in making it as smooth a transition as possible. You've laid the groundwork for Galactic Mail's success moving forward."

Costa waved his hand in a small gesture.

"If you control the computers, Ms. Dawson, you control Galactic Mail. There's a lesson there for you, I think. But I knew immediately it was over when the computers told us you were the legal CEO of Galactic Mail. I'm still surprised, mind you. I had no idea there was an independent oversight of Galactic Mail, or why or how it might be triggered. But I knew it was over. At that point, there is no sense in not being gracious. I've been with Galactic Mail almost thirty-five years, and I always wanted what I thought was best for it and the people in it."

Dawson considered. Costa's access to the corporate VR and mail system had been restored, though without CEO and command privileges. She decided, and triggered a mail through the VR. She sent him Jan Childers' introduction to the role of Watcher.

"To your point about the independent oversight, Mr. Costa, I have something you might want to VR. I think it's important, and may be helpful. I've just sent it to you. I'll be happy to wait."

Costa got a bit of a distracted look as he accessed his mail in the VR, then became unfocused in the way typical of someone in full immersion VR.

When he came out of the VR, Costa looked down at the floor between them for several minutes. Dawson waited. Finally, he looked up at her.

"Some members of the Board brought up these objections, of course. I ignored them. I was convinced it was both improper and unnecessary for Galactic Mail to stand aside and simply watch these travesties unfold. On Wallachia. Other places. Having accomplished Jan Childers' grand objective, putting an end to interstellar war, Galactic Mail should now put an end to tyranny and despotism. I was convinced I had the vision to carry that out, to extend Jan Childers' legacy.

"Padma Kosar is exhibit number one that that was not the case. And not just her. There will always be concealed vipers around, waiting, plotting, scheming. As Jan Childers knew, and as I have learned to my sorrow.

"Jan Childers herself is exhibit number two. Even she could not see how to go on to that next step, how to put an end to the minor tyrannies, without putting in place a much greater one. And she truly did have vision, enough to see me coming, to see Padma Kosar coming, two hundred years ago, and set her plan in place to stop me.

"Thank you, Ms. Dawson. This has all been very humbling, that VR perhaps most of all. To be lectured by Jan Childers herself in just how wrong I was –"

Costa shook his head. He took a deep breath, and let it out slowly, before continuing.

"So now what, Ms. Dawson? What would you have me do?"

Dawson hadn't been sure which way she was going to jump. It had all depended on Costa. Now, she knew.

"Stay on at Galactic mail. On my staff. Emeritus CEO. Adviser to the CEO. Whatever you want to call it. Introduce me around. Be a sounding board for me. One thing you have that my staff does not have is experience, with the people, with the institution. Don't take that out of Galactic Mail. Use it."

Dawson waved her hand at the office around her.

"Stay here, in this house. We'll be moving the corporate headquarters to Kalnai, and the region manager and division manager will still live in the other two houses. But this house will be empty, and it's just a hop away from Kalnai. Commute a couple days a week, overnight. Or two weeks a month. Or something. Bring Vivian along rather than be apart if you want. I'll permanently assign a VIP courier ship for your use.

"Or you can move to Kalnai. Specify your own arrangements. But I want you on the executive staff, and Galactic Mail needs you."

Costa looked at her sharply, and she nodded, once. He looked around the office, and his eyes drifted out the window, to Galactic Mail's massive base and its sprawl of buildings. Having shrunk before, he seemed to draw himself up once again.

"I'll have to talk to Vivian, see what she wants to do. We've been happy here. It's a tempting offer, Ms. Dawson. I'll seriously consider it, and let you know."

"I can't ask for more than that."

Dawson stood up, and Costa followed suit. They shook hands, more earnestly than they had during the ceremony, and went back outside to see to their guests.

The Extent Of The Rot

Dawson was back on Kalnai, relaxing with Morgan over a private breakfast. The kids were off with Grandma to see some local museum in Slenis, Kalnai's capital, about fifty miles away over the mountains to the north.

"Wait. You're going to keep Sylvain Costa?" Morgan asked.

"Yes," Dawson said.

"In your inner circle?"

"I suspect so, yes."

"In God's name, why? Wasn't he all the trouble to begin with?"

"Yes, he set the policy," Dawson said. "But he sees now it was that very policy that attracted the snakes. Like Padma Kosar. But the depth of his contacts and experience is not something you just throw away. It was part of the advice about dealing with the upper management, in the materials for the Watchers, from Jan Childers herself. Win over whoever you can, and kill the ones you can't. Don't leave anyone to plot against you. But don't waste experience either."

"Bloodthirsty ancestor you've got there."

"She never killed anyone she didn't have to, and when she did, she did it quickly. But she didn't believe in half measures."

"So what's on your schedule now that you're back?" Morgan asked.

"Check in with Micheli, check in with the forensic team, check in with research. See where everybody is at. And I need to start putting a real staff together. This is all running me ragged."

"Assign that to Jack. Let him pull the executive staff together."

"Good idea. I guess check in with him is first."

"Yes, Ma'am. You called?" Turner asked

"Hi, Jack. Have a seat," Dawson said.

Turner plopped into a chair in front of her desk.

"How're things going?" Dawson asked.

"Pretty good. The remains of the Board is all back on the planet. A bunch of them went back home until the next Board meeting. Most of the rest will be leaving soon. All of the strategic resources have been sent back to their normal stations, except for a last-ditch defensive sphere of twenty thousand drones we retain here around Kalnai until things shake out."

"And mail and freight operations?"

"All good. The regions and divisions pretty much run themselves, and they're still doing it."

"All right. I have an assignment for you. I probably should have given it to you a couple weeks back. I want you to head up the search committee to fill out the corporate headquarters staff. See if a few of the remaining Board members will help out, and get Micheli's chief of staff, Dev McConnell, to help as well.

"Oh, and I got a mail from Sylvain Costa this morning. He's accepted my offer to be Adviser to the CEO. So when he shows up, use him on this as well.

"Go through all of the higher-level personnel in all of the divisional and regional staff. Look for people with competent seconds who can step up. Use the computers to search personnel files. You can use the prior organization chart as your guide as to what we need."

"Got it. What about Security?"

"Well, we still need a security function, but I think someone having been in Security here before is probably a negative. So is applying for and being seriously considered for a job in Security here. I don't know what to do about that. Come up with some ideas for me to consider."

"Got it."

"Speaking of security, what happened with the existing Security forces at the other regions and divisions?"

"Well, I've been looking at the preliminary findings coming out of the forensic accounting team, and it looks like the rot was spreading out from Doma. Kalnai was the biggest freight operation of all four regions, including Doma, and Kosar concentrated here and on the other two regions, Odla and Pulau, though they were a bit smaller than Kalnai and Doma. Kwan replaced Security commanders in the eight smaller regions as well, and they were starting to have an effect on the divisions, but that was still filtering down, and it was hit or miss.

110

"So we haven't had any problems with divisions. Some of the regions have been dicey, and I'm still worried about Odla and Pulau. The demise of Padma Kosar and your peaceful transition with Sylvain Costa quieted down Pulau, but Odla is another matter."

"The divisions, then, may be where you have to look for untainted security people to staff a true security department once again. As for Odla, do we need to go there?"

"I don't think it would hurt. I can't put my finger on it, but it sounds to me like Mauro Ikeda is in trouble."

"Like his communications are being filtered?"

"Or like he knows they're being monitored. Yeah. And the Security chief there is one of Kwan's hand-picked hardliners."

Dawson called up the layout of the base on Odla in VR. The Security Building was off to one side of the complex, but not all the way across the field as on Kalnai or Doma.

"All right. Let me think about it. More meetings first. Get started on staffing."

"Yes, Ma'am."

Dawson visited Micheli in her office. The redecorating required by Kian Sitko's spectacular demise had been completed for over a week, but a faint odor of fresh paint hung in the air.

"Come in, come in, Ms. Dawson."

The secretary left and pulled the door shut behind her as Dawson walked across the office to where Micheli waved her to the seating arrangement off to one side of the desk.

"Hi, Kali. How're things going?" Dawson asked.

"Good, actually, Pat. At first we had a little trouble with Security in a couple of divisions. Your orders relieving all the chiefs of Security of their commands in the Kalnai region had spotty results. But when first Myron Kwan and then Padma Kosar were removed, either people stepped down voluntarily or their juniors helped them along. So we got back full control over our own regions and districts. We're now reviewing the performance of the district commanders to see if some of them can be reinstated or take over in the regions. The regional Security commanders were all tainted. So say the accounting folks, anyway."

"What about your friends in the Pulau and Odla regions? Turner said there might be some problems in Odla."

"I worry about that, too," Micheli said. "The mails from Ikeda don't sound right. They're all text-only, which is a change in itself, but they are also just a little off. Like –"

"Like he's trying to let you know something's wrong without coming right out and saying it and getting in trouble."

"Yes. Exactly."

"All right," Dawson said. "I see George and I are going to have to pay a little visit to Odla. But everything in Kalnai region is good?"

"Yeah, we're doing fine. No need to worry about us."

"OK. Off to see the forensic accounting team. Thanks, Kali."

"Well, we have several topics to talk about. Which would you like to hear about first," Hwan Cooper asked.

Cooper was the head of the team, and had brought several other people to the meeting.

"Don't care. Up to you. But let's keep it to executive summaries for now. I'll read your detailed reports later," Dawson said.

"OK. Let's start with the funding of the warships. Sean, you're up."

Sean Pema arranged his notes, then activated the display through the VR.

"The first thing to notice is that, while there is a large amount of money involved, it is not enough to build sixty warships from the keel out. I conclude therefore that these warships already existed, and were perhaps refitted for use by Security. Based on the pricing we regularly see on ships in this size range, this would be more than enough money to completely refit sixty existing ships," Pema said.

"So somebody took a bunch of ships out of mothballs and worked them up," Dawson said.

"That is correct," Pema said. "So one question right off is, Where did the ships come from? We found no separate payment for the ships themselves, so we conclude they either came from the location that worked the ships up, or they were Galactic Mail ships in the first place."

"Let me guess. They were Galactic Mail's own ships."

"Again, correct. They were removed from a fleet of ships that were mothballed nearly a century ago. They had been in storage, one might say, in distant orbit around Doma's sun."

"Which means Doma refitted the ships, because without refitting they weren't spaceworthy enough to get them to anywhere else, and you can't tow them."

"You're very good at this game. That was our conclusion as well, so we looked for where the payments went. It's pretty easy to track down the flow of a large amount of money, and this wasn't really that hidden. It was listed as ship repairs, but there was no commensurate addition to the normal flow of ships in the operational inventory that were undergoing refitting or repairs on Doma during the time period, and the ordering and payments were not handled through purchasing and accounts payable as they normally should be."

"Do we know who was involved in the project?"

"On our side, it would have had to include at least the corporate controller or the head of accounting or, more likely, both."

"OK. Well, they're both dead, so we can't ask them. How about on the Doma side? Was the government involved in this?"

"Oh, yes. The Secretary of Trade appears to have been the main conduit. The orders were issued to vendors by his company, rather than by Galactic Mail purchasing, and the payments were made directly to his company from a blind account outside of the accounts payable process. The Prime Minister was likely also involved. Large contributions were made to her election funds from the same blind account, which she used for her own election campaigns and the election campaigns of other members of her political party."

"Were those payments out of the range of historical amounts?"

"Yes, and they were contemporaneous with the ship refitting project."

"Are the current officeholders the same people who were bribed?"

"Yes. The government hasn't turned over since these activities."

"Got it. Sounds like I need to have a little talk with some people on Doma. Among other things, it sounds like it's more than time for the government to change. What's next?"

"Mariana Petrov has the internal skimming project," Cooper said.

Petrov switched the screen, and a list of names and amounts showed up on screen.

"Padma Kosar was making regular additional payments to her high-ranking subordinates. Here we see the amounts paid over the last fifteen years to each of them, as well as the percentage of their regular Galactic Mail salaries that were being paid as additional side payments during the period each person received these payments."

"Wait. You're telling me she was paying these people two to five times again their legitimate salaries?"

"In direct payments. That's correct."

"That's a lot of money."

"Not in absolute terms. The number of people getting these side payments was small, but they were strategically selected. She could command absolute obedience from these people, both because of how much she was paying them on the side and because they knew she had records of the payments made."

"So she could destroy anyone who stepped out of line."

"Correct. And without implicating herself. She took pains to obscure where the payments were coming from inside the company, but not to whom they were going."

"And what about Padma Kosar herself, and Sylvain Costa?"

"That's a separate effort," Cooper said. "Gene, your turn."

Eugene Rudaski switched the screen to a tabulation of his results. Dawson spoke first.

"Wait. That can't be right."

"Oh, it's correct," Rudaski said. "It's surprising, perhaps, but it's correct."

"Padma Kosar took no inappropriate funds out of Galactic Mail? At all?"

"Not that we can find. And we went over her books and accounts with a fine-toothed comb. Including her bank records, for which she kept the password on her computer account at work. She's clean as the driven snow."

"Power was its own reward."

"Apparently so. Not so for Sylvain Costa, but there's an anomaly there. He was being paid by Kosar, in some pretty large amounts, but he didn't take any inappropriate funds himself. Further, he kept the funds Kosar shifted to him sequestered from his own finances, and never touched them."

"He took the money to humor her. She wanted a lever on him."

"That could be. He never used them. Any additional funds Kosar shifted to him he put in a separate account, and never touched any of it. One more thing. He donated the total amount in those accounts to the families of those killed in the destruction of the Administrative and Security Buildings on Doma."

"I'll be damned. An honorable man. In the middle of a snake pit, to be sure, and terribly wrong on policy, but not a cheat, not a thief. And he gave it all back before we even did the audit."

"That's correct. He currently holds no expropriated funds from Galactic Mail. At all. None. And he never spent any of it. Not even the interest it accrued. It was all given back. And his personal accounts, which he sent to us on his own, by the way, are clean, clean, clean."

Dawson turned to Cooper.

"Thank you very much. That's all I need for now. And thank you, everybody. I'm looking forward to reading your detailed reports. And don't dumb them down for me. I'm an accountant myself."

And with that, Dawson was off to her next meeting.

New Capabilities

Dawson met with Austin Misra in her conference room in the wing of the Administrative Building she was borrowing from Micheli. He brought two other members of his team with him. One carried something covered with a black cloth and set it on the table.

"As you'll recall, Ms. Dawson, during our very first meeting we discussed the smaller munitions we had developed, and you asked us when we might have some of our less potent explosives deployable – the concept being that a ten-megaton warhead was a bit of overkill for most real-world situations."

"Exactly. Well stated," Dawson said.

"Thank you. We believe we are ready to go with the first of your requests, a device to implode a building while minimizing damage to nearby structures."

"I could have used a couple of those a couple of weeks back."

"So I understand. Unfortunately, these things take time. However, we are ready to go with one, and we have a couple of samples."

"How does it work?"

"The concept is simple enough. It's basically a very tiny nuclear shaped-charge demolition, deployed four to a warhead for a small missile. Sort of a nuclear claymore, if you will. Drop one in the center of each side of the building, aimed toward the center, and they bring the building down."

"How tiny is tiny? We are talking a nuke here."

"It's a variable yield device. From one-half ton to five tons of TNT equivalent, as opposed to multiple kilotons or megatons. You set it for the yield you want."

"And four of these tiny nukes come down on the building?"

"Not exactly. The issue with that is the building may be five or ten stories high. To bring the building down, you really want to cut off its legs and let its own weight bring it down. The best place for the munition then is in the basement, but penetrating multiple stories of the building is a problem for a small projectile. What we do instead is bring the weapons down in the ground very near the side of the building. Depending on how deep the basements are, we can detonate it at different depths. The deeper the better. It holds the explosive against the building. Then we blow in the basement wall. High-velocity debris from that takes out the interior supports."

"What's to keep the whole thing from just blowing straight up into the air?"

"The munition itself is in a heavy canister that is open on one side. I have a little model here."

Misra took the cloth cover off the model on the table. It was the size of a five-gallon bucket, with a four-inch-wide slot cut in its side for about a third of its circumference.

"That's the nuke?"

"No, this is the containment."

Misra reached inside the slot and pulled a cylinder about the size of a twelve-ounce drink bottle out of the middle of the canister.

"This is a model of the munition."

"That's it? That's the nuke?"

"Yes. As I say, it is a tiny device. Very low yield, as nuclear explosives go."

"And that canister's enough to hold a nuke?"

"A tiny nuclear device, for a very short period of time, yes. That's all we need to direct the charge. it doesn't have to be impenetrable, just harder than the side of the building's basement."

"Which is concrete."

"Which is concrete. The containment is gold-titanium alloy. Gold-titanium alloy is four times stronger than steel, at about two gigapascals. Good structural concrete is at best 50 megapascals."

"Forty times as strong as concrete?"

"Yes. It's been very effective in testing."

"No doubt. Do the munitions all go off at once?"

"No, they're staged. Actually, they all go off at the same depth, but the impacts are staged, so the munitions arrive and detonate in a circle. If they all went off at once, the center of the building might be blown up into the air or the walls blown out to the sides by the combined over-pressure in the basement. Setting them off in a circle, in sequence, rocks the center of the building in a circular pattern, and pulses the overpressure. That assists the implosion."

"Wow. And this works?"

117

"We believe so. We don't have any big buildings no one is using at the moment to try it out on, but the testing we have been able to do, on concrete walls and such, has been in line with predictions."

"But it won't take out the whole city or something?"

"No. The failure mode is likely to be that it won't take the building down. It will still not be a nice place to be when the building gets hit, though, even if the building doesn't come down. The overpressure pulse within the building from the initial device will be fatal to anyone in the building."

"What about radiation?"

"It's not really a problem. As I say, it's a very tiny device, and it has been designed to be clean even so."

"Understood, Dr. Misra. And you have two of these missiles for me at the moment?"

"Loaded on *Quicksilver* and ready to go, Ms. Dawson."

Dawson's last meeting was with George Enfield.

"We need to go to Odla. Something's up over there," Dawson said.

"Problem with Security?" Enfield asked.

"I think so. Vissente Van Laar is one of Padma Kosar's hardliners. And communications from Mauro Ikeda are off."

"Off?"

"Wrong somehow," Dawson said. "Micheli can't put her finger on it, but there's been no video, and his text-only communications are not like his normal. Like he's trying to signal something, but doesn't want to push the envelope too hard."

"Got it. OK. When you want to go?"

"How about after a decent night's sleep? First thing tomorrow?"

"Works for me."

Taking Odla

As they were on the shuttle up to the *Quicksilver*, Dawson told Enfield she had sent a mail to Ikeda the night before telling him she was coming to pay a visit.

"Are you sure that was wise?" Enfield asked.

"If you want to gather up the mice, put out the cheese."

"Rats in this case."

"I suspect so," Dawson said. "We have to know. We can't leave him there, to strike at his leisure. Van Laar will probably think this is his big chance. How lucky can he get?"

"Hopefully not luckier than us."

"Just check your rig before we go down to the planet."

Once aboard *Quicksilver*, Dawson met with the specialist on the little missiles, Bill Rodriguez. They were in a single container in one of the *Quicksilver*'s three weapons racks, the other two holding beam weapon drones. They would also be taking ten full hunting parties – a hundred drones – with them to Odla, but they would remain in hyper, at the drones' hyperspace-1 limit, and she wanted some ready-access firepower along in orbit.

"OK, so this is the building we might have to take down," Dawson said as she pushed the base map and building plans to him in VR. "I think we want to use the smallest setting on the wall toward the rest of the base, bigger on the sides facing away from the other buildings, and small again on the side opposite from the other buildings, so we don't throw debris toward them, but I'll leave the exact settings up to you."

Rodriguez considered the plans in VR.

"Not a problem. I can dial this in, I think. I take it you want me to err on the low side."

"Well, we're going to be down there, in this location," Dawson highlighted the map. "So, yes, a little finesse would be appreciated."

Rodriguez chuckled.

"I understand, Ma'am. Easy does it. No problem."

On the way to Odla, Dawson prepared some command files and some recorded messages. She also reviewed the personnel files of the security people as well as the people in the regional manager's office.

When they got to Odla, she was ready.

Their shuttle landed on the roof of the Administrative Building. They were met by a young woman in civilian office wear.

"Good afternoon, Ms. Dawson, Mr. Enfield. I'm Mr. Ikeda's personal secretary. If you will please follow me."

As the secretary led them into the building, Dawson logged into her account in the Odla computer systems. She had checked it and Enfield's from orbit, and they were uncompromised. She thought. She signaled to Enfield through the VR.

Dawson to Enfield: Not Ikeda's secretary per files.

Enfield to Dawson: Note stance, walk. She's Security.

Dawson to Enfield: Facial match. Security. Armed agent.

Dawson tapped into the security video feed from Ikeda's office.

Dawson to Enfield: Ikeda's office. Two right, two left, officer in the near left corner. No body armor.

Enfield to Dawson: How about the fainting scam?

Dawson to Enfield: Sure. I'll take the right.

They were shown through the executive offices, which were awfully quiet at the moment, as the secretary kept up a light patter. At Ikeda's inner office, the secretary opened the double doors wide. and motioned them in. They could see Ikeda seated behind his desk, looking out the side window of the corner office.

Dawson and Enfield walked through the double doors into the room. Both doors closed suddenly behind them, and there were two armed agents on either side, about eight feet away, guns drawn and pointed at them.

"Freeze!" a security officer in the corner said.

At finding themselves in a trap, Dawson's eyes rolled up into her head and she fainted. She fell bonelessly, like a puppet whose strings had been cut, twisting as she fell. Enfield jumped back to be clear of her fall, while rotating to his left. With all five of the Security people watching Dawson fall, he hit the release on his holster, raised the pistol and opened fire.

Security's attention turned back to Enfield as he started firing, but as Dawson fell face first onto the floor she rolled onto her back and opened fire, having hit the release on her holster as she fell.

Enfield double-tapped the two guards to the left, and Dawson double-tapped the two guards to the right while lying on her back on the floor, holding the gun above her waist and shooting over her knees. Enfield then shifted his aim to the officer in the corner behind the two guards, who had belatedly gotten his gun out of the holster and was raising it, and shot him through the head. The doors started to open and Dawson shot past Enfield and hit the secretary just behind and under the point of her chin, the perfect head shot from her floor position. The secretary's gun clattered to the floor.

The Security people did get off two wild shots, but neither hit Enfield or Dawson.

Dawson got up from the floor, walked over to where one of the four Security people was moaning, and dispassionately shot him in the head.

Dawson and Enfield both reloaded and put their half-empty magazines in the empty position, then holstered their weapons.

"Are you OK, Mr. Ikeda?" Dawson asked.

Ikeda didn't answer, and Dawson walked over to the desk and checked on him.

"He's cold. Refrigerator cold. Bastards killed him and they took his body out of the fridge to use him as a prop."

Enfield touched the chair.

"Chair's cold, too. They probably just wheeled him in, chair and all. Well, that's why his mails seemed off. He wasn't writing them."

"OK. Well, two can play rough."

Dawson triggered one of her command files on *Quicksilver*.

Enfield walked over to the Security officer.

"This Van Laar?"

"No, that's Nakano, his second in command. I can see Van Laar in his office in the VR. He's trying to figure out why his video from Ikeda's office cut off just after we walked in the door."

Dawson looked out the side window of the office. The view though the main picture window behind the desk was of the shuttle field, but the side window looked out toward the Security Building barely eight hundred feet away.

"Come on, let's get into that inner office. I want to get away from these windows."

"Wait. You're going to nuke *that* building? We're right on top of it."

"All the more reason not to be next to the windows. They're reinforced, but even so. Come on."

They went through the double doors, walked past the body of the secretary, and took a sheltered position behind the secretary's desk in the outer office.

"So now what?" Enfield asked.

"I sent a message out over VR in Mr. Van Laar's voice, from his account, calling all his people to muster in the Security Building."

"Won't Van Laar countermand that?"

"He's cut off from VR, and locked in his office."

"How can he be locked in his office?"

"He has his door rigged so he can lock it from his desk, but the easiest way to do that is to use the computer system. He should have put in a dedicated circuit. I wouldn't have been able to take it over."

Dawson watched Van Laar try again and again to unlock the door with the switch under his desk, and finally resort to pounding on the door.

"He's pounding on the door now. But that won't help. He made sure his staff couldn't open it from the outside."

Dawson and Enfield both got a warning ping in the VR. They lay on the floor and covered their heads with their arms.

The shuttle trip had been timed so *Quicksilver*'s orbit would put it overhead for their first hour on the planet.

The small missile came in ballistic after the initial two-minute burn got it started. It shed its nose cone at five thousand feet and deployed its four warheads. They spaced themselves out both horizontally and vertically by using their steering flaps and dive brakes as they targeted the ground on the four sides of the Security Building. They adjusted their orientation with finicky precision as they fell, ensuring their blast directions were aligned toward the walls of the building. Each impacted a foot away from the basement walls, penetrated to a depth of twenty feet, and detonated, in succession.

Each explosion blew in the basement wall in the sub-basement, turning tons of concrete into blocks of shrapnel that took out supporting columns not intended for lateral loads. Each explosion also rocked the building away from it, especially the larger-yield strikes on the longer front and back walls. Each explosion, after the microseconds it took the containment to fail, shot dirt and gravel straight up into the air and excavated a half-round crater against the side of the building.

The Security Building stood for several seconds, and then in slow motion fell in on itself into its ruined basements.

The Administrative Building shook to the series of four explosions. As soon as they were over, Dawson jumped to her feet and ran into Ikeda's inner office, looking out the side window. She saw the Security Building hesitate, seem to shudder, and then collapse.

Enfield walked up behind her.

"Well, that's impressive. Didn't even break the windows."

"Dr. Misra will be happy. Just like he planned it."

"Do you think anyone is still alive in that mess?" Enfield asked.

"No. The pulses of overpressure in the building from the explosions would have killed everyone even before the building collapsed."

They watched for a few minutes as fire spread through the debris, and the dirt and gravel that had been shot into the air fell like rain around the destroyed structure.

"This is the fourth building I've taken down with all hands in the last three weeks. I'm getting really tired of this," Dawson said.

"You didn't have much of a choice. It's like I asked you a month ago. How ruthless are you prepared to be?"

"I know. But I think my ruthless is running out."

Dawson took a deep breath and let it out slowly.

"All right," she said. "Let's see if any of Ikeda's headquarters staff survived the brief reign of the late chief of Security."

Dawson set the computers to reviewing the surveillance tapes to determine where the headquarters staff was. The answer hit her hard.

"Oh, God," Dawson said, and sat heavily in one of the side chairs of Ikeda's office.

"What?" Enfield asked.

"Ikeda's inner circle – his chief of staff, second in command, secretary, all of them – were being held in the basement detention area of the Security Building. They're all gone."

Dawson looked out at the burning wreckage of the Security Building, then around Ikeda's office, at the six bodies laying in expanding pools of blood, the blood splatter on the walls, and the bloody mess on the ceiling of the short entry corridor.

Enfield sat in the other side chair.

"Pat –"

Dawson looked at Enfield with tears in her eyes.

"Just tell me this will all be over soon. I'm getting tired of being the angel of death, wreaking destruction wherever I go."

She closed her eyes, and tears slid down her cheeks.

"I can't guarantee that, Pat, but I do think we're getting to the end of it. Never lose sight of the goal. We need to keep Galactic Mail from becoming a galactic tyranny. With what we've seen so far, we were closer than we thought. Mad Empress Padma was right around the corner. It's been a near thing. But I think most of the large-scale destruction is probably over."

Dawson nodded at him, wanting to believe. She heaved a huge sigh, then wiped the tears from her face and eyes angrily.

"OK. Pity party's over. Let's go rescue anyone I haven't killed."

With the small detention area in the Security Building full, the rest of the headquarters staff had been held in a large area in the basement of the Administration Building. Dawson and Enfield went down to the basements to release them. The guards who had been set at the locked doors had left in response to the fake call from Van Laar to report to the Security Building, and had likely also been killed in Dawson's attack on Security.

In contrast to the regional administration, the division offices on Odla were largely unaffected. The division manager had kept her head down and acquiesced to Van Laar. Turning a blind eye to his excesses had saved them from his wrath, and the division staff and headquarters were intact.

Dawson made the division manager the acting manager for the region pending the results of Turner's staffing effort, and she and Enfield headed back to Kalnai.

Unfinished Business

It was several days later Turner reported to Dawson on their progress in staffing up the new corporate headquarters on Kalnai.

"It's going really well," Turner said. "When we first started, I couldn't believe the magnitude of the job. But I was looking at it all wrong. Sylvain told me to worry about the department heads, and let the department heads work on their own staffing issues. Not to try to do the whole thing myself."

"Costa's been a help, then?"

"He's been great, Pat. First thing, he knows absolutely everybody. At least that's what it seems like. Second, he knows all the subtleties of those personnel records. It turns out there are all sorts of little key words and phrases that have hidden meanings. If it says, "Performs flawlessly in his current position," what it really means is, "Don't promote this guy, he can't do the next job up." How would you know that? But Syl knows that and all the other little subtleties. And third is, he works his ass off. You always think of the big shot as somebody who just sits around, but this guy's not afraid to work, and he's fast."

"So what's our status, overall?"

"We have recommendations for most of the department heads for you, as well as department sizes required, office space required, that sort of thing. We're refining those now. We should have a full package within a week."

"All right. Good. How much would it hurt you if I borrowed Costa for a day? I have some unfinished business on Doma to attend to."

"We'll miss him, but a day won't impact that schedule. We'll queue up anything that needs his touch until he gets back."

Dawson, Enfield, and Costa took a shuttle up to the *Quicksilver* for the trip to Doma. They could have made the trip aboard the GMS *Cheetah,* the fast courier ship Costa and his wife had been commuting on, but *Quicksilver* still mounted the second nuclear demolition missile. Dawson didn't know if she'd need it, but the first one had come in handy. Better safe than sorry.

Sylvain Costa had arranged the meeting with the government of Doma. They had been asking for a meeting since Dawson's kinetic strike on Galactic Mail's Doma headquarters three weeks before.

After decompressing and showering off the skin protectant required by the acceleration tanks, Dawson dressed in her best business suit. She met with Enfield, Costa, Marine Gunnery Sergeant Gul Murphy, and Bill Rodriguez, Dr. Misra's nuclear demolition specialist, in the captain's ready room.

"This is the building I want you to target. Aim to take the whole building down. Send George and me both a health check every fifteen minutes. If neither of us answers within five minutes of the check, take the building down. If either one of us answers, you go another fifteen minutes."

"Are you sure about that, Ma'am?"

"Absolutely sure. Can do?"

"Yes, Ma'am."

"Are you sure that's necessary?" Costa asked.

"Nuking the building? No. Taking preparations to nuke the building? Absolutely. You said they wanted to talk to me about the kinetic strike on our Doma headquarters. They may even want to take me prisoner as a war criminal or some such bullshit. The only reason that strike was necessary was they consorted with Padma Kosar. And they did it for money. I'm after justice."

"The angel of death rides again?" Enfield asked.

"If I have to. This is one bunch I am going to take no grief from whatsoever. Speaking of which, are your men ready to deploy, Gunny?"

"Full battle rattle and dressed for the party. Yes, Ma'am."

The shuttle set down on the shuttle pad on the roof of the five-story wing of the executive office building in downtown Nadezhda. A group of half a dozen men, obviously security types, came out of the doorway that led into the office spaces on the sixth floor beyond. They had a weapons scanner and other accoutrements of the trade.

They were a bit nonplussed when the shuttle door opened and disgorged a dozen Galactic Mail Marines in powered armor and full combat load-out, including heavy plasma rifle, shoulder-mounted rocket launcher, and spinal mortar. Fully anonymous within their completely blank helmets, they formed a security cordon for the Galactic Mail delegation, edging the Doma security men aside with, "Excuse us. Make way, please," from their chest mounted speakers.

Dawson, Enfield, and Costa walked through the cordon and past the Doma security men into the offices on the sixth floor of the building. They passed down the hall to the main conference room and walked in.

"Ah, we're all here. Good," Dawson said as the three Galactic Mail attendees walked down the table and took their seats.

From Galactic Mail files on the government of Doma, Dawson recognized Prime Minister Helen Utkin, Foreign Minister Monica Jin, Finance Minister Dmitri Katsaros, Justice Minister Alexandra Fiala, and Trade Minister Horace Duncan.

There were no introductions. Utkin dove right in.

"Marines, Ms. Dawson?" Utkin said.

"When greeted at the door by your armed goons, Ms. Utkin? I was just returning the favor. Had you met me at the door like a proper host, you wouldn't even have known I had them along," Dawson said.

Utkin flushed with anger at Dawson's content and tone, as well as her use of the common form of address rather than the 'Madame Prime Minister' proper etiquette required, but she said nothing.

Instead, the Justice Minister took the floor.

"We're here to discuss the flagrant violation of Doma law in the kinetic bombardment of Doma by forces under your command, Ms. Dawson, including the cold-blooded murder of over one hundred thousand Doma citizens. That is a war crime for which you must answer."

"Actually, no, I'm not here to talk about any of that shit."

"Ms. Dawson! This is a heinous crime you cannot just shrug off."

"Sure I can. It's right in the site agreement for Galactic Mail. You might take the time to read it at your leisure, Ms. Fiala, rather than waste all our time proving you have no idea what you are talking about."

"The site agreement does not say you can bombard the planet."

"The site agreement says Galactic Mail's internal affairs are Galactic Mail's business, and are not subject to review by the Doma government. The locations I hit with two kinetic strikes were both completely within the Galactic Mail site. I did not bombard the planet, as you put it."

"You killed a hundred thousand people."

"In order to stop Padma Kosar from detonating two ten-megaton thermonuclear warheads, and killing three million people on the Galactic Mail site and millions more here in Nadezhda."

"So you claim."

"You were provided with the complete conversation between me and Padma Kosar, and recordings of the two warheads being found on the Galactic Mail site, Ms. Fiala. Or do facts hold no sway with an attorney such as yourself?"

"You will answer for this crime, Ms. Dawson."

"Oh, I have answered for it. Just now. Go ahead and read the transcript of your surveillance video later if you need to review. If you have any remaining questions, please, get in touch.

"Right now I would like to move on to the topic of conversation I am here for, which is the provision to Padma Kosar, by this government, of sixty warships, which were deployed against the planet Kalnai in an interstellar incursion. Such incursions are not permitted by Galactic Mail."

Duncan, the Trade Minister, spoke up.

"If Galactic Mail wishes to purchase warships, or drones, or any other materiel from our industrial sector here on Doma, that is its right. What use its employees make of such materiel once it is delivered is outside of our control."

"Ah, Mr. Duncan. How nice of you to speak up. You knew very well the transaction was irregular, and not a normal materiel acquisition."

Duncan reddened and answered with real anger.

"I knew no such thing. The accusation is preposterous. You come in here, with your Marines, and your arrogance and rudeness, and you shrug off the murder of a hundred thousand people. And now, to deflect from your heinous crimes, you accuse us, with no evidence, of being a party to a procurement irregularity? That's, that's – It's ludicrous on its face."

"Ah, but there is evidence, Mr. Duncan. The transfer of the orders through your personal company rather than through regular channels, the transfer of funds from a blind account rather than from Galactic

Mail accounts payable, and the price itself, which was so far over market as to constitute a substantial bribe for your involvement."

Duncan pounded his hand on the table, stood, and flew into a rage.

"You're insane. No such thing happened. You will not deflect us from making you answer for your crimes, you monster!"

Duncan reached inside his coat jacket and started to draw a pistol from a shoulder holster. Dawson had dropped her right hand below the table as soon as he stood up. Her 8mm pistol fired twice as soon as it cleared the edge of the table, two shots to the center of mass. Duncan fell heavily backwards, and both he and the chair continued on to the floor.

Dawson and Enfield, now with his pistol in his hand as well, stood up and turned to the left to cover the entry. It was only a few seconds before security agents burst through the double doors.

"*Halt!*" Dawson said.

The agents, hearing that command voice and seeing the two pistols aimed at them, hesitated.

"Don't even think about it," Dawson said.

Dawson swung her pistol down and to the right, to point directly at Utkin across the table.

"Order them to stand down, Ms. Utkin."

"You wouldn't dare," Utkin said.

"I've killed two hundred thousand people so far this month. What makes you special?"

Utkin looked down the slide of the Vandar, into Dawson's eyes, and saw the steel purpose there, the grim determination to do what had to be done, regardless of the cost. On Odla, Dawson had seen in herself the angel of death. Now, on Doma, Utkin saw it in her, too.

"Captain, stand down, please. We can handle this."

The security men withdrew, closing the double doors behind them.

"You will never get out of here alive, Ms. Dawson," Utkin said

"On the contrary, Ms. Utkin. When we have finished our business here, you will personally walk me out to my shuttle. Or else a dozen Marines with plasma rifles will burn their way in here looking for me. Failing that, I have a ship in orbit. If I don't answer a health check by radio every fifteen minutes, they have orders to nuke this building from orbit."

"In the middle of a city?"

"Oh, they're very small nukes, Ms. Utkin. But they will take down this building and kill everyone in it. I know. Three days ago I nuked a building this size on Odla, less than three hundred yards from where I was standing. I watched it fall. I'm not sure how many people were in it at the time. We never did get a final count."

"You're a monster."

"Oh, please, Ms. Utkin. After you sold sixty warships to Padma Kosar? After you arranged your little assassination attempt?"

"What? What are you raving about?"

"Do you think the implications of Mr. Duncan having a pistol here in the executive office building were lost on me, Ms. Utkin? With your screening procedures, he could only have had that pistol if you personally approved it. Why would you do that, eh? Planning a little extrajudicial proceeding? And don't tell me you were surprised when he staged his little show of outrage and then tried to draw his pistol on me. I'm far better at reading body language than you are at hiding it.

"As for the sixty warships, do I need to go into details about each of the payments made to you and your political party? How Galactic Mail money funneled to you through a blind account by Padma Kosar was instrumental in your party fighting off a serious challenge in the last parliamentary elections? How those payments were timed to coincide with each of the acquisitions she made from you in building her little private navy?

"Padma Kosar kept copious records, Ms. Utkin. Even if Ms. Fiala here has no interest in seeing those records, I bet her counterpart in the shadow government would be positively thrilled to see them. Not to mention the press.

"Oh, and if I don't respond to that radio check from my ship, and they do nuke this building, they will also transmit the complete financial records and statement of audit to the shadow government and the press.

"No, Ms. Utkin, I'm not a monster. From your personal point of view, I'm much worse than that. I'm an *accountant*."

The fire had gone out of Utkin as Dawson talked, and she seemed to shrink into herself as the implications sank in. The scandal would be horrific, her reputation ruined. The government would fall, and the opposition party would take control, perhaps for decades. Everything she had worked for all her life, in ruins.

"What would you have me do, Ms. Dawson?" Utkin asked.

"I think you should retire from government service, Ms. Utkin. For health reasons, I think. You don't look at all well. And your little legal beagle here. And your money man, too. By the way, that was a really nice job shifting all that money around, Dmitri. If we weren't looking for it, we wouldn't have seen it."

Katsaros, the Finance Minister, blanched.

"And the financial records?" Utkin asked.

"Well, were you three to retire from politics, Ms. Utkin, oh, say in the next two weeks, I don't really think they would hold much interest for anybody. I certainly wouldn't have any interest in publicizing them. I'm sure your party, and the nation, would thank you for your years of service, and wish you well in honored retirement. With their majority, your party would elect a new prime minister from among their number, and that new prime minister would select a new cabinet.

"Why, were you all to retire, I wouldn't even bring up the Galactic Mail money that somehow found its way into all three of your private accounts. It should be a very comfortable retirement, indeed."

"What guarantees do we have?"

"None. But then again, I am not the one here forsworn, Ms. Utkin."

Utkin stared down at her hands on the table for several long minutes. While they were waiting, Dawson and Enfield holstered their pistols. Utkin really had very few options. Finally, Utkin sighed and looked up at Dawson, still standing.

"Very well. You leave me very little choice, Ms. Dawson."

"That was the general idea, Ms. Utkin. Oh, and one more thing. Doma will no longer be the corporate headquarters of Galactic Mail. It will remain a regional headquarters, but this government has proved itself unworthy to host the company."

"You can't unilaterally change the site agreement," said Jin, the Foreign Minister.

"I am not unilaterally changing anything, Ms. Jin. Ms. Utkin is going to sign an amendment to the agreement, which I have brought along with me."

Costa, who had sat silent through the whole meeting, produced from the breast pocket of his jacket two copies of a one-page amendment to the site agreement, removing the requirement that the

Galactic Mail location on the planet be the company's corporate headquarters. He handed them to Dawson, who set them in front of Utkin. Utkin saw they were already signed by Dawson. Utkin signed both copies, and slid one copy back across the table to Dawson. Dawson handed it back to Costa, who put it back in his jacket breast pocket.

"A pleasure doing business with you, Ms. Utkin. I am sorry to hear that health issues are forcing your retirement, but a quiet retirement is much less stressful to one's health than the hurly-burly of politics, particularly with a potential scandal in the wings.

"And now, if you would accompany me to my shuttle, Ms. Utkin. I'm sure I've taken far too much of your valuable time already."

The Galactic Mail attendees walked down the table to the doors leading out to the shuttle. Before she opened the doors, Dawson turned to Utkin, standing beside her.

"Smile and wave, Ms. Utkin. Two hundred thousand Galactic Mail employees died during Padma Kosar's grab for power. You got off easy."

Dawson opened the doors, to find the security people nervous as pregnant cats in the hallway between the conference room and the Marines outside. Ever the professional politician, Utkin smiled, and even managed a laugh, as they walked down the corridor and out to the shuttle.

Dawson, Enfield, and Costa boarded the shuttle, and the Marines withdrew their security cordon and boarded. The shuttle pilot spun up the engines, and they headed for *Quicksilver* in orbit.

Dawson turned to Costa.

"You see? No problem. I told you I could negotiate an amendment to the site agreement," Dawson said.

"Remind me never to negotiate with you, Ms. Dawson," Costa said. "And thank you for these active ear plugs. I certainly didn't expect a shoot-out over the negotiating table. That was the most remarkable thing I have ever witnessed. Still, you let her off the hook."

"I must be learning that you can't just kill everybody. Monica Jin was actually squeaky clean, completely uninvolved. The others were collaborators, but they saw it primarily as a way to advance their party interests, which they see as the nation's interests. The truly guilty party, Padma Kosar's right-hand man in the Doma government, was Horace Duncan. Duncan was a greedy pig who was in it purely for his own enrichment. And he did not walk out of the room."

When they got back to Kalnai, it was Friday afternoon. For the first time in a month, Dawson took the weekend off.

Delayed Mail

On Monday, Dawson was back in her office on Kalnai and catching up on mail. Scanning down her overflowing in-box, and feeling overwhelmed, her eye caught something and stopped dead in its tracks.

It was a mail from Jan Childers. The sent date was one hundred and thirty years ago, and contained a large VR file. Dawson opened the VR file, and was once again on the porch of Campbell Hall on Horizon. She looked out at the small town of New Hope, on the broad plains between the forested hills and the river, and her heart ached with longing.

She turned to her left, and Jan Childers sat there as before, aged and white, with her blanket on her lap and her cup of tea on the table between them. Childers turned toward her, and she was once again transfixed by those eyes.

"Good morning, Mister or Madame CEO. I am Jan Childers.

"This mail has been set to be held by the computer systems of Galactic Mail until certain conditions are met. Those conditions have been fulfilled, and that is why you are now finally getting this mail.

"Those conditions include that the Watchers have successfully asserted control over Galactic Mail and pulled it back from the path to totalitarianism. Those conditions also include that the current CEO is one of the Watchers, installed by the new Board as part of the clean-up process, and that process has concluded. Galactic Mail is now settling back down into the routine of running the day-to-day affairs of the business.

"May I say first, Congratulations. We are not sure now, as I record this, if the Watchers will be able to successfully assert control over Galactic Mail or not. There are too many variables, too many possible scenarios, too many possible chains of events to be at all sure. We have done everything we could to help you in this effort, the planning, the documentation, access to the computers, to the training. Everything we could to increase your chances of success. But the probabilities people I have had consider the question always come back with fifty-fifty odds, which is a very precise way of saying they simply don't know.

"But the fact that you have received this mail means that you have succeeded, against whatever the odds, and so, once again, I say, Congratulations. You did it, and, no matter whose descendant you are in the multiple chains of Watchers we have set, I personally am very proud of you all.

"Now I come to the purpose of this mail. Having achieved your purpose, against all the odds, you now find yourself in control of a huge organization. I suspect at this point, you are simply feeling overwhelmed. You were plucked out of whatever life you were leading, first to watch over Galactic Mail, and then to assert control over it, to right its course. You have fulfilled all your ancestors' dreams to have accomplished such a feat, and it may now be time to go home."

Childers paused for a moment before continuing.

"If your heart leapt when I said that, then I have read my tea leaves correctly."

Childers smiled, and picked up her cup and took a sip of tea. She set it back on the table.

"Having succeeded in pulling Galactic Mail back from the plunge into totalitarianism, you now find yourself in a position for which you have neither the skills nor the experience to be successful.

"When I founded Galactic Mail, it was much smaller than the organization you are now heading. A few million people. Nevertheless, I already had for over a decade headed up the largest military organization in human space. Subsequent leaders of Galactic Mail probably did as I did, coming up through the ranks, shouldering the responsibility for larger and larger portions of the company, learning the leadership and delegation skills required to be successful in heading up such a huge organization.

"No one who did not come up through the ranks of Galactic Mail has those skills. In particular, you do not have those skills, as you are probably realizing.

"So I just wanted to point out to you that your huge responsibility is ended. You have succeeded. You have my heartfelt gratitude, and that of all of the Watchers' ancestors.

"You should not feel like you are abandoning our trust in you, or leaving the job half finished, or walking away from your responsibility, if you step down now as CEO. Far from it. You set aside your life, left your home world, ignored your family, underwent whatever hardships, took terrible risks, made difficult decisions. It is likely that many people have died, many at your own hand, or at your command, in the fight for control. And that weighs heavily on you.

"I know. I've been there, and I know."

Childers paused there, and her eyes once again struck Dawson. The eyes of someone used to wielding tremendous authority, yes. But more than that, those eyes reflected the burdens of that authority, and the regrets. The feeling that, if she had been that little bit better, her own ghosts would perhaps be less numerous. Dawson saw the authority there, as before, but now she also saw sympathy, and more, understanding.

"You did all that, took those risks, made those fraught decisions, and you succeeded. You have forced Galactic Mail back onto the straight and narrow path of ensuring peace while avoiding tyranny.

"Your sole remaining responsibility is to ensure that the leadership of Galactic Mail has the skills and experience it needs to lead the company going forward.

"The Watchers remain the Board of Directors for now. They can continue to exercise oversight over the new management for the next five years. They will be replaced over the next ten years – the next two shareholders meetings – with new directors, per the by-laws. But it is the responsibility of this Board, at this time, to find within Galactic Mail the leadership it needs to be successful.

"Once more, to you and all the Watchers, Congratulations. Job well done. I am so very proud of you all.

"For you, Mister or Madame CEO, it is now time to step down, to take back your seat on the Board of Directors. Attend Board meetings, of course. Make sure the new leadership stays on the correct path, of course.

"But it is time now to go back home, to your family, to your life.

"And thank you, from the bottom of my heart."

Dawson sat for a long time there, on that porch, Jan Childers beside her, looking out at the town of New Hope. She felt like a huge weight had been taken off her shoulders.

She looked back at Jan Childers, now in an end-of-recording loop, looking out at New Hope and slowly rocking in her chair. She had seen the future. No, more than that, she had dreamed the future as it could be, and made it happen. She had forged it with her own hands.

And now she had given her seventh great-granddaughter, Patricia Dawson, permission to go home.

Stepping Down

Dawson asked Enfield to a private dinner in a small meeting room off her office that evening. When Enfield arrived at her office, a waiter met him at the door and showed him into the inner room. The table was set for dinner for four, with fine china, wine glasses, and candles. A wine cooler stood to the side next to a catering cart, and another server was preparing a tossed salad on the cart.

"Wow. What's the occasion?"

"We're celebrating. Have a seat," Dawson said as she waved him to a chair.

"We expecting guests?" Enfield asked as he took the indicated seat.

"Yes. In a moment. First things first. I have a little announcement to make. I am stepping down as CEO of Galactic Mail."

Enfield just stared at her.

"The job is done. The job we set out to do. I've just pushed you a mail I received this morning. You should view it. I'll wait."

Enfield's expression settled into the blank look of someone in immersive VR. After several minutes, his attention returned to the here and now.

"That woman never ceases to amaze me. She saw all this coming. She's right, of course. It just never occurred to me," Enfield said.

"Or to me. But she's right. And I'm going home."

"Who should we install as CEO in your place? Do you have a recommendation?"

"Yes, actually. Sylvain Costa."

Enfield started at that.

"Reinstall him as CEO? The guy who was the problem in the first place?"

"Yes. With Micheli as his chief of staff and heir apparent. He finishes out his original term, then Kali takes the helm. We'll still have the board then, as it will be right before the next shareholders meeting."

"That could work. We get the continuity, Micheli gets, what, four years in the number-two spot, then takes the helm for ten years. And we know where she's coming from. I like it."

"And I like that I get to go home."

Just then, the waiter reappeared and showed Bob Morgan and Tatiana Khatri into the room.

"Did you start the party without us?" Morgan asked.

"I was told this was a surprise party," Khatri said.

"It's a surprise, all right," Enfield told his wife. "Pat just told me she's stepping down as CEO of Galactic Mail."

Khatri and Morgan both turned to Dawson.

"Our job is done," Dawson said. "We're going home."

The dinner was wonderful.

Costa tapped on the doorway to Dawson's office.

"You wanted to see me, Pat?"

"Yes, Syl. Come on in and close the door. Have a seat."

Dawson waved him to a chair in the side seating arrangement and they both sat. It was unusual for Dawson to close her door, and the staff knew not to bother her if it was closed.

"I wanted to tell you something, and I need to ask you a question."

Dawson looked down, and settled her hands in her lap. She looked back up at Costa.

"I'm stepping down as CEO of Galactic Mail. The job I came to do is done, and I now find myself in a position for which I have neither the skills nor the experience to be successful."

"I'll admit it is a handful, even for someone who came up through the ranks."

"Which leads me to my question. The Board has asked me for a recommendation for my replacement, which, as you say, should be someone who came up through the ranks.

"My inclination is to recommend you to finish out your last appointed term, with Kali Micheli as your chief of staff and heir apparent, to replace you at the end of your term. I was wondering if you would be open to that."

Costa said nothing. He was struck silent, as if someone had sucked all the air out of his lungs. Dawson simply waited. When he finally recovered, he spoke with deliberation.

"I will say it was deeply disappointing to be removed so abruptly, in the middle of my term. It was a personal failure. Not going out on top, not completing my term. I would appreciate the opportunity to finish the job, cap off my career successfully, and lead Galactic Mail down the road Jan Childers chided me about in that VR you shared."

"The road you had departed from."

"Yes, although I was following in the direction my predecessors had pointed us. That's part of the problem. I can see now we need much more education, and continuing education, about what Galactic Mail is, and what it must remain, for all employees. It would be good to have everyone in Galactic Mail view that VR of Jan Childers once a year, for one thing."

"It would require you to move here to Kalnai. Doma will not be the headquarters."

"I understand. Vivian has been coming with me on these trips, and she likes it here. She loves the mountains. At worst, it's four years to a remote posting before returning to Doma. We've had those before as well."

"Is all that a 'Yes' then?"

"Yes, Pat. Ms. Dawson. I accept, if the Chairman sees fit to nominate me and the Board concurs."

Patricia Dawson officially communicated her resignation as CEO of Galactic Mail to George Enfield as Chairman of the Board in a mail the next day. That triggered a whole bunch of things to happen in rapid succession over the next twenty-four hours.

Jack Turner also communicated his resignation as vice president.

Natasha Sanna, age 91, and Juan Linna, age 88, communicated their resignations as members of the Board of Directors.

The Board, now down to fourteen members, voted via mail to reinstate Patricia Dawson and Jack Turner to their Board seats, bringing the board back up to the sixteen-member complement authorized by the by-laws.

George Enfield, who remained Chairman, named Sylvain Costa as CEO, and the Board concurred via mail.

Sylvain Costa made Kali Micheli his vice president and chief of staff.

The board also voted affirmatively by mail on a motion to provide the former CEO Patricia Dawson the standard retirement package for retiring CEOs of Galactic Mail, despite the fact she had only held the post for a bit over five weeks.

PRESS RELEASE
– For Immediate Release –

SLENIS, KALNAI – Galactic Mail has announced the move of its corporate headquarters from Nadezhda, Doma, to Slenis, Kalnai. The firm already maintains a large regional headquarters on Kalnai. The new corporate headquarters will be built on the company's existing site fifty miles south of the capital of Slenis.

Kalnai is the company's largest regional hub, and is closer to the population center of its service area. The move will make the company more responsive to customer needs by shortening communications paths from the headquarters to its regional and divisional locations.

Galactic Mail's corporate headquarters had been located on Doma, thirty miles east of the capital of Nadezhda, for its first one hundred and eighty-five years, even as the population center of its customer base moved over a thousand light years toward the center of the galaxy

GALACTIC NEWS SERVICE
***** Breaking News *****

GNS–Slenis, Kalnai. Galactic Mail has announced that Sylvain Costa has been reinstated by the Board of Directors as its chief executive officer. This is widely taken as a sign among corporate observers that the turmoil that has engulfed the company for the last month is beginning to die down.

Stepping down after only five weeks at the helm is Patricia Dawson, an accountant and investigator, who, it is widely believed, was brought in by Galactic Mail's Board of Directors to investigate irregularities within the company centering around the actions of Padma Kosar, Costa's former chief of staff.

The internal power struggle for control of Galactic Mail, which apparently did not involve Costa, devolved into military operations between groups within the company loyal to Dawson and Kosar.

Major military actions occurred within the last month on Kalnai, Doma, and Odla, three of its major regional locations.

Ultimately Dawson's forces wrested control of the company from forces loyal to Kosar, who was killed in a kinetic strike on the former corporate headquarters on Doma. An estimated two hundred thousand Galactic Mail employees died in the corporation's internal war.

The company's mail and freight services were unaffected by the turmoil.

GALACTIC NEWS SERVICE
***** Breaking News *****

GNS–Nadezhda, Doma. In an unexpected move, Helen Utkin, Prime Minister of Doma, has announced that she is stepping down and retiring from politics. She cited health reasons for her resignation. It is widely expected that Foreign Minister Monica Jin will attempt to form a new government.

Finance Minister Dmitri Katsaros and Justice Minister Alexandra Fiala also stepped down, to provide Jin the opportunity to form her own cabinet. They also announced their retirements from politics.

The resignations come just a week after the suicide death of Trade Minister Horace Duncan. Duncan was found dead in his office within the executive office building. It was not known how he had secreted a firearm into the building.

Horizon

Patricia Dawson scrambled up the last few feet to the peak, a rocky outcropping at the top of a foothill of the mountains rising to the east. She turned around to the west, looking out over the trees toward New Hope. She could see Campbell Hall and its grounds below her, on a lower hill closer to the city. She watched as a large freight shuttle took off from the New Hope Spaceport, taking containers of freight or resupply up to a Galactic Mail ship somewhere in orbit.

Galactic Mail. Wherever you looked, there it was.

It was only six weeks since she had been on a passenger shuttle, headed up to the GMS *Mnemosyne* in orbit. How much had changed. Not New Hope, or Horizon. It was she who had changed, who carried those changes around inside her.

She had wrestled with titanic historical forces, run the largest company in human history, commanded a space fleet in battle, directed kinetic and nuclear strikes on three planets, killed two hundred thousand people with large-scale weapons, most of whom, truth be told, had been innocents caught in the wrong place at the wrong time. She had killed over a dozen people herself, up close and personal, with the handgun she now carried everywhere. Most of them had simply been following orders.

And she had won. She, and George, and Jack, and the rest of the Watchers. Kali Micheli, and yes, even Sylvain Costa. They had pulled humanity itself back from the brink of an apocalypse most people had known nothing about, still knew nothing about, and probably never would.

There was still work to do. What system could the Board devise to pull Galactic Mail back from the brink next time? They had the copious notes and staff work from Jan Childers and her fellow founders. They also had the experience of having done it once already, an advantage Jan Childers had not had. The work on that had not yet begun.

The Board had to keep an eye on Sylvain Costa. So far so good. He had distributed the initial Jan Childers VR recording to all Galactic

Mail employees with the request to watch it and take it to heart. He pledged to do more to build a culture within Galactic Mail that enshrined the ethic of hands off internal planetary policies, however benighted.

He had also proposed, and the Board approved, a reinstatement of Galactic Mail's longstanding, but since abandoned, policy of transporting refugees away from trouble spots to planets willing to take them. The human right of people to leave, to emigrate, would once again be enforced.

Of the twenty-four systems in which Sylvain Costa and Padma Kosar had intervened, nine had begun the path toward a better system, while fifteen, including Wallachia, had sunk back into despotism. On the hundreds of other worlds where revolutionary movements had been emboldened by Galactic Mail's policy under Costa and Kosar, dozens of governments had resorted to kinetic bombardment of their own people once the Board rescinded the policy.

There would be local despotisms, but no galactic tyranny. She and the other Watchers had fulfilled Jan Childers' mandate and rescued her legacy.

Having done all that, Patricia Dawson found it impossible to go back, to take up the reins of her life as it had been. Accountancy for local companies did not now stir the interest it once had. Instead, she would concentrate on her position on the Board, which would run for the next ten years.

Money was no worry. The Board of Directors received a generous stipend, with a generous retirement to follow. Either was more – much more – than she and Morgan had both made before her involvement with Galactic Mail. The additional retirement the Board had decided was due her as a former CEO of Galactic Mail was much larger still.

On moving back to Horizon, her mother had made her an offer. To swap houses, trading their little suburban house for Campbell Hall. Dawson had insisted on paying the substantial difference in value, but her mother had demurred. She said she had all the funds she needed, and, besides, the house was a family heirloom, intended to be handed down at the proper time. The maintenance and upkeep on the huge house had simply grown too much for her, and the small suburban house would be a relief. Also, the suburban house was closer to her "man friends" in town. Never having remarried, her mother maintained an active social life into which Dawson had been careful not to inquire too deeply.

As the sun passed into mid-afternoon, Dawson set aside her wool-gathering. She checked her watch. Time to be heading down to Campbell Hall if she wanted to be home when the twins got home from school.

They would want a snack.

Made in the USA
Monee, IL
08 April 2021